THE
BURNING
SKY

T.V. Olsen

FAWCETT GOLD MEDAL • NEW YORK

A Fawcett Gold Medal Book
Published by Ballantine Books
Copyright © 1991 by T.V. Olsen

Library of Congress Catalog Card Number: 91-91893

ISBN 0-449-14691-X

Printed in Canada

First Edition: August 1991

CHAPTER ONE

THE BLOOD BAY GELDING HAD A WILY INTELLIGENCE SU-
perior to any that Brightlaw had ever seen in a horse. The
animal had cultivated a neat habit of standing placidly, almost as immobile as a statue, until a man got atop him and
the gate of the branding chute was swung open.

Then he'd launch himself out to the corral, exploding into
action like a gigantic jackrabbit. Nobody could keep a firm
seat on "Old Bloody Bay" for more than a few moments,
but in that brief time he could easily get hell pounded out of
him.

First Sergeant Michael Hanrahan watched with undisguised satisfaction as Trooper Seth Brightlaw was dumped
into the dust for the third time. A couple of other troopers
ran out to grab the prancing blood bay before he could tram-
ple his fallen rider.

Brightlaw crawled painfully to his feet, and this time he
was limping slightly. You son of a bitch, he thought calmly
as he met Hanrahan's mocking gaze.

He was fully aware that the sergeant hated his guts. Hanrahan was the son of immigrants who had come from the old
country to Boston while Michael was still a small boy. Being
Irish and Catholic, they had been treated like dirt. Sergeant
Hanrahan would know enough from just a glance at Brightlaw's pre-military record. He was more than happy to inflict
his hatred on any upper-class Bostonian of English descent.

Now, leaning with his burly arms crossed on a corral pole
as he watched Seth Brightlaw crawl up out of the dust, Han-

1

rahan was grinning. He was a thick-bodied man, gravel-voiced and stogie-puffing, somewhere in his thirties. His square, tough face was deeply weathered and bisected by a thick red mustache.

He took the cigar out of his mouth, idly tapping ash from its tip.

"Well now, Trooper. That's what I call an engaging encounter between horse and man. Would ye be terribly discommoded if I asked you to do it for me one more time? Just to see, ye understand, if we can work a bit more vinegar out of the animal."

Brightlaw didn't have a hell of a lot of choice.

Since he had joined the U. S. Cavalry, he'd been treated to a series of indignities that he couldn't have anticipated. An enlisted man might be subjected to just about any kind of crap that his noncom superior chose to inflict. By and large the higher-ups of the command, the commissioned officers, were somewhat more compassionate. But dealing with a prejudiced noncom, a first sergeant of your troop, could be a lot different.

That's how it was in this troop. Hanrahan had had it in for Seth Brightlaw from the start, and he wasn't a damned bit shy about letting everyone know it.

Seth Brightlaw slapped his dusty hands on his pants and gave his best friend, Trooper Max Pulvermacher, a wry glance.

Like a lot of other enlistees in the cavalry, Pulvermacher was a foreigner. Ironically, as a native of Bavaria he'd fled his native land to escape being a conscript under the kaiser's military law. Yet an odd combination of circumstances had caused him to wind up in the U. S. Cavalry. Brightlaw wasn't clear on all the details, for Max was mostly a secretive man.

Pulvermacher was short and stocky, with a thatch of pale, short-cropped hair and whiskers and a ruddy, boiled-looking face that had a deceptively sleepy look. His usual manner was ponderous and slow-moving. But whenever he did speak, what he said was worth hearing.

Max was leaning against the corral poles, as were Hanrahan and other men of the troop. Now he closed one eye in a kind of solemn wink. It was on the side away from where Hanrahan was standing.

Somehow the gesture lent Seth Brightlaw a spark of strength that enabled him to say cheerfully, "Of course, Sarge. Pen him up and I'll bring him out again." He seasoned it with his best Harvard accent, knowing that that would rile Sergeant Hanrahan more than anything else.

Naturally Hanrahan would pretend otherwise, and did. "Ah, me bucko," he purred, flicking more ash off his stogie. "There's the spirit. That's what I like to see in my boys. Very well, lads. Haze the brute back in the chute. . . ."

The horse-handlers led the now docile blood bay into the branding chute and dropped the gate to confine him. Brightlaw managed to swing himself atop the chute.

He and the other horse-handlers had gone through hell trying to work the rough edges off Old Bloody Bay. They'd spend hours leading him around the corral roped by the neck, bringing him suddenly against the snubbing post. Later they'd fastened a tow sack on his back and let him try to buck it off. Later still, though there was little indication that the animal would accept a back burden, they'd tried a saddle on him. The blood bay had merely turned canny. At each session he'd be completely tractable until a rider hit the saddle. The horse would have been scrubbed long ago, except that Hanrahan enjoyed disciplining his men this way. Seth Brightlaw was, of course, his prime target for discipline.

All of it trickled through Brightlaw's tired brain as he stood astraddle the chute above the blood bay.

It was hotter than Hell's hinges—what you'd usually expect at high afternoon on this vast wasteland called the Mojave Desert. Brightlaw's sweaty clothes clung like wet rags to the bruised soreness of his body. And waiting for him was the instrument of still another savage pounding.

Best if you don't think about it. Just do it.

Brightlaw lowered himself into the saddle. He felt a coiled quiver of anticipation run through Old Bloody Bay's muscles.

"Very well, gentlemen," he said in his finest affectation of a crisp Harvard accent. "You may 'let 'er rip.' "

The handlers hauled open the gates. The blood bay boiled into the corral, erupting into its usual pile-driving lunges. Brightlaw had been through it enough times to know how the ride must inevitably end. Sometimes, in the past, he had taken a deliberate dive from the animal's back, making it look as if he'd been pitched off.

Not this time, he thought grimly. He had taken it too often.

Goaded to stubbornness—maybe because his brain was too numbed for any sort of clear thinking—Brightlaw meant to stick the ordeal out to the bitter end—if he could manage to. What was it, something he was trying to justify to himself? To Hanrahan? To his fellow troopers?

Right now he didn't give a good goddamn. Hang on. Just hang on!

Brightlaw had never been much of a horseman in his boyhood. But several years of working with the U. S. Cavalry had enabled him to hold his saddle seat fairly well.

He kept his body alternately braced and slackened, rolling to the blood bay's violent pitching. Even though he tried to take each jolting impact by keeping his body as limp as a dishrag, he felt as though his spine might wrench apart from the brutal poundings.

Some cavalry people thought that a horse was about the dumbest critter in all creation. Others, that it was one of the smartest. Brightlaw leaned toward the latter opinion. Since the first of his encounters with Old Bloody Bay several weeks back, he'd become accustomed to a variety of the animal's techniques for unseating or damaging a rider.

Coming out of his pile drivers, the big gelding switched suddenly to sunfishing. Brightlaw was prepared for it, shifting his weight to the right as the animal's left shoulder dipped. The blood bay twisted high and came down. Again Brightlaw was ready, throwing his weight the other way as the horse shifted leads. The animal let out a squeal of rage as his rider refused to be thrown. He sunfished again and again, and each time Brightlaw managed to shift his center of balance.

With fine instinct the blood bay launched himself toward a corner of the corral. Brightlaw was braced for either a spin-around or a deliberate attempt by the animal to smash the fence flank-on. He suddenly sensed it would be the latter, and jerked his right leg free of the stirrup, swinging it high just before the collision. The horse's rump slammed against the poles with a force that shook the whole corral. Wheeling now, he raced for the center of the enclosure, wheeled again, and lunged for the fence at an opposite angle. Brightlaw had barely gotten his right foot securely back in its stirrup. Now he had to kick his left foot free. Again came the crashing impact that would have crushed his leg had it remained between fence and horse.

The blood bay raced around the corral now, bucking in loose circles and figure eights. Then he went on the pile drivers again, plunging up and down stiff-legged. His fore-hooves struck the ground ahead of his hindhooves.

Brightlaw had never stuck on Old Bloody Bay anywhere near this long before. Now he realized that his own stubborn pride had betrayed him. God, I'm no bronc-buster! His body was being snapped back and forth, his spine whiplashed on each leap. Sky and earth, along with the faces of the watching troopers, gyrated crazily in his blurred vision.

With the calculated precision of a seasoned bucker the blood bay started to "pioneer" now, changing direction at every plunge. Calling up the last of his failing energy, Brightlaw tried to anticipate the animal's calculations, bracing and slacking his body just so.

But it was hopeless. The battering shocks sent blood surging to his head. Suddenly he felt it gush from his nose.

"Hey there, man! Take a dive. He's too damn much for you. Take a dive!"

Dimly Brightlaw knew the drawling voice, now lifted to a shout. It came from Idaho Bitters, one of his fellow troopers who was watching from outside the fence.

Right now it seemed like particularly good advice. Bright-law could feel an actual weakening of his pain-wracked muscles. On each plunge his body was flung backward, then forward.

On the next pile driver Brightlaw let his body go wholly loose, leaning out from the saddle so that the jarring impact threw him off. He hit the ground and rolled over and over until his body slammed against a corral post.

He lay stunned, unable to move. Then he felt the grip of hands as his fellow troopers hauled him out of the corral.

CHAPTER TWO

OLD BLOODY BAY HAD PROMPTLY CALMED DOWN. HE stood quietly, his red coat burnished by the afternoon sun, and shook his black mane and tail as he gazed wickedly at the troopers. He pawed the ground with one forehoof, as if challenging any of them to try it again.

Brightlaw climbed groggily to his feet, assisted by Idaho Bitters and Max Pulvermacher, one on each side of him. His knees felt as weak as water.

"Hey, Seth," drawled Idaho. "You oughta taken a dive 'fore you did. Reckon you can stand all right?"

Idaho was tall and slim and gangling, with a pair of wispy, straw-colored mustaches that he'd curried neatly down either side of his lean jaws. His usual whimsical, show-nothing expression only slightly masked a real concern for his friend.

Brightlaw nodded.

He was about to add a word of assurance when Sergeant Hanrahan came tramping up, grinning around his stogie. "Now," he said mildly, "that was a bit o' topping of a steed such as I've rarely seen. So finely done that I'd admire to see it done again."

"Sir?"

"Ye don't 'sir' a noncom," Hanrahan said in the same mild tone. "Could it be the ride mucked up your fine Boston wits a bit, bucko?"

"Possibly it did, Sarge." Brightlaw's head was still spinning, and he still felt wobbly on his legs as Idaho and Max let go of him. "Do I understand that you wish me to mount the animal again?"

"Ah. Ye apprehend me perfectly." Hanrahan grinned. "It would seem a pity, after you've ridden the beast so nobly, longer than anyone has, and have broken his spirit so far, that ye not finish up the job? Time to strike is *now*, while the iron's hot."

Brightlaw stared at him, almost disbelieving. Why you son of a bitch, he thought. You hate me more than I could have guessed.

He couldn't find an immediate response, but Max Pulvermacher spoke up with his usual ponderous calm. "Sergeant, I do not think this is so good an order. Seth is done up. And the horse does not look so tractable yet."

"Dutchy, nobody asked your goddamn opinion," Hanrahan barked menacingly. "Did they, now?"

"*Nein*, Sergeant," Pulvermacher said stolidly. "I am only saying the truth."

"Your *opinion*, ye mean, Dutchy darlin'," Hanrahan grinned. "To which you're always entitled, of course. . . . Well, Private Brightlaw? Would it discommode you too frightfully to attempt mounting the beast again?"

He has you by the balls, Brightlaw thought dismally.

If he were to refuse, or to plead inadequacy of any sort, Hanrahan would have won this round. It was a personal challenge that Hanrahan, not he, had created. The human body would take only so much at one time. Another try at the blood bay in his present condition might well leave him permanently incapacitated.

Brightlaw could only stand silent, fumbling for words as he weighed the wicked triumph in Hanrahan's face. It was his own unbending pride against Hanrahan's unyielding hate. And he had no words at all. . . .

"Sergeant Hanrahan!"

The exclamation came from Private Sparling, who had just hurried up.

Alfred Sparling was the fort commandant's personal "striker," a prissy and officious type who didn't fit in much of anywhere except to run errands for a commissioned officer. The regular troopers referred to him as a "dog robber." Sparling was short and fat and had protuberant pale eyes.

Hanrahan whipped the stogie from his mouth. "Aye!" he barked impatiently. "What is it, Alfie?"

"Colonel Traviston wants you and all personnel of your troop to report at once to headquarters. Your new troop commander has arrived, and the colonel wants you on hand for the welcome."

"Oh, shit," Hanrahan said with weary disgust, dashing his cigar to the ground. "All right. Another crapping captain, I'd expect."

"No." Sparling beamed. "Just a first lieutenant. But I'd hustle my hocks over there on the double, if I were you. Look alive, Sarge!"

He bustled officiously away.

"Damn little pismire," Hanrahan grumbled after him, then raised his voice to bawl out orders. One trooper was to summon the men on the hay-harvesting detail, another to round up the farriers and vets, and so on. "The rest of you assholes repair to your barracks and try to curry yourselves into something like honest-to-God soldiers. Dismissed!"

Brightlaw, Idaho, and Pulvermacher fell into step as they headed across the dusty parade grounds toward their barracks.

None felt exceptionally set up by the prospect of a new troop commander, although his being a lieutenant rather than a full captain was the subject of mild curiosity. Most likely he'd be a younger man (the steeper chain of command came with age and tenure). And, of course, the troopers were always concerned with how much of a martinet any new officer might prove to be.

Under the Tables of Organization for the cavalry, a full regiment was supposed to embrace twelve troops of about eighty men each. A troop was to include one captain, one first lieutenant, one second lieutenant, one first sergeant, five line sergeants, and hence down the line through corporals and privates. But any given troop in the Army of the West was hardly ever up to full strength. Usually each troop had to make do with whatever it was assigned.

At Fort Burnshaw, this remote outpost in the Mojave, the only three troops of the regiment were lucky to command more than a dozen apiece at any one time. It was a desolate post to begin with, and the desertion rate was close to one third of enlisted personnel per year.

Nobody in the command gave much of a damn. Just about each man, from the top officer down through the ranks, was simply hanging in for his own reason. Why not? It was a pretty easygoing way of life, except for that amount of drill and field service necessary to keep the garrison on battle alert. And each man was usually assured his full monthly pay in any case. You could depend on the army.

"Ho ho!" Max Pulvermacher said with mock enthusiasm as they trudged along. "What do you think of this, *mein herrs*? Maybe a real gutsy shavetail we will get! He will be raring off to perform valorous deeds, eh?"

"Shouldn't bother a fuckin' draft dodger like you a whole lot, Dutchy," Idaho drawled. " 'Bout time you got to see some real action."

Pulvermacher threw back his head, braying out a full-throated laugh.

Brightlaw, lurching along between his two closest buddies, smiled only a little. He was beaten so sore and lame that he could barely navigate. That's why they were sticking so close beside him. But like them, he did feel an uneasy curiosity about the new troop commander.

Captain Milgrave, the head of B Troop and its only commissioned officer, had died suddenly a month ago of a combination of alcoholism and kidney disease. A development that had deeply pleased First Sergeant Michael Hanrahan, because Captain Milgrave had borne down hard on him. It was standard procedure for the troop commander to come down hard on the sergeants, for the sergeants to lean on the corporals, for the privates to catch hell from just about everybody.

So it wasn't likely that the arrival of a new troop commander would change much of anything for the better. Yet Hanrahan, a mere noncom, had been running the troop solely to his taste for a month now. It would be good, Brightlaw thought wearily, to have even that much pressure off his back . . . no matter what the new lieutenant might turn out to be.

He couldn't have guessed how wrong he was.

Inside a half hour the men of B Troop were more or less washed and shaved and curried. They were assembled in loose formation in front of Colonel Traviston's headquarters.

The arrival of a new commissioned officer at a post was usually an occasion for mild ceremony. It didn't mean a hell of a lot, except for the more practical aspect of "ranking out of quarters"—meaning that an officer could gain access to lodgings that were superior to those of anyone of lesser rank. Even so, the quarters on any frontier post were generally so crappy that any increase in comfort was of minor degree.

The three understaffed troops were arrayed on the parade ground, each at inward-facing angles. Seth Brightlaw chanced to be in the first line of the front-facing troop.

Brightlaw was sweating and stiff-shouldered, aching all over and a little sick from the heat in his wool uniform coatee, and wishing to God it was over with. He wondered for the thousandth time what madness had caused him to enlist in the Army of the West.

In an objective way, of course, he knew. A lot of circumstances had led him to it, one after the other. No man alive could predict what would be the result of any particular action he committed. So here he was, like it or not.

Idaho and Pulvermacher were on either side of Brightlaw, lending him a kind of moral strength, for they knew what he'd undergone from Sergeant Hanrahan's special treatment. Hanrahan himself was now standing in front of the troop with a kind of ramrod-straight braggadocio. *He* was the real leader of this troop, his stance seemed to declare, and any new CO had damned well better not forget it.

Finally the front door of the headquarters building swung open. Three people came out.

Seeing two of them, Brightlaw felt a sick shock run through him. But he kept facing straight front, full of an iron determination not to let any of his reaction show.

Colonel Lewis Traviston barked a loud "Ahem!" and clasped his hands behind his back. He was a pompous and pot-bellied little clown with bushy gray burnsides and sweeping walrus mustaches.

"Men," he declared sonorously, "I wish to introduce the latest arrivals to our garrison. These are First Lieutenant Philip Umberhine and Mrs. Umberhine. Lieutenant Umberhine will be the new commander of B Troop. He is an experienced and seasoned officer who will . . ."

Colonel Traviston went on in the same rambling vein. But Brightlaw barely heard the words. His gaze was riveted on the two people who stood beside Traviston. He felt a thickening in his throat and was vaguely aware of more sweat crawling down his ribs under the wool coatee.

There they were. Phil Umberhine and his lovely wife. The man and the woman who had driven him to this lonely outpost, where he should have been least likely to ever encounter either of them again. And here, by some twist of fate, they were.

Both of them had noted him, too. They were staring at him, though not very obtrusively. Marlee Umberhine's face revealed only a hint of the surprise and dismay she felt. And Phil couldn't quite conceal the wicked, undisguised pleasure he felt.

It showed on the genial white grin below his trim black mustaches.

CHAPTER THREE

ONCE THEY HAD BEEN FAST FRIENDS. IT HADN'T BEEN ALL that long ago, and yet it seemed like another lifetime, another world.

Seth Brightlaw, Phil Umberhine, and Marlee Benton had grown up in the same well-to-do neighborhood above Boston Common. They had come from the same social strata, upper-middle-class, and their folks socialized together a lot. Each of them was a conventional product of his or her class, and different from their schoolmates only in having a maverick streak of mischief in their natures.

Phil was a couple of years older than either Seth or Marlee, and he had been the leader in their childhood games and pranks. Even back then Phil had possessed an innate streak of cruelty that wasn't yet fully cultivated, but which he enjoyed taking out on his close but younger and slighter friend, Seth.

Like Sergeant Hanrahan, Phil was a born bully. Today, Seth Brightlaw could think back on the old days with mingled pity and anger. God or Fate or whatever had left something out of the bullyboys. They were unfinished human beings, in a way. Nobody was perfect, but most people had a built-in compassion that balanced out their unfavorable traits.

Back fifteen years ago, however, Seth had idolized his older friend without reservation. Phil was big and burly and handsome, aggressive and daring, always ready for a romp or a ruckus. Seth had always followed his lead and so (within the well-defined limits of propriety) had the tomboyish Marlee.

None of their infractions of the rules was terribly serious. They might ''coon'' apples from a neighbor's orchard or tip over an outhouse or play hooky from school. Practically every kid got involved in something of the sort once in a while. But Seth and Phil and Marlee would carry their pranks to ingenious extremes, and it set them apart from the others.

They grew out of it, naturally, as they got older. Seth came to resent Phil's pushiness. And Marlee developed into a lovely young woman, for whose favors both boys began to contend.

They were all in their teens when Phil Umberhine got a West Point commission that the district congressman, a close friend of his father's, was able to obtain for him. Seth followed his own father into the legal profession, enrolling in Harvard Law School. Marlee, meantime, went to the finest of finishing schools to round out her education as a Boston debutante, all of it to culminate in an elaborate coming-out party.

For a short while Seth Brightlaw had been exultant. Phil would be isolated at the United States Military Academy in New York—a comfortable distance from Boston. Phil might expect a little vacation time on holidays, but it wouldn't be enough to enable him to get back home by rail or stage and then make the return journey. The only time he could expect any real leeway for a visit home was during the summer, maybe a month or so. That left Seth Brightlaw, attending law school in Boston, on the same turf with Marlee Benton. And he had courted her ardently.

There were no objections from their parents. Seth was socially ''right.'' He was as acceptable a suitor as Phil Umberhine would have been. So Phil, able to get back to Boston only a month out of each year, should have been at a distinct disadvantage.

It turned out that he wasn't. Phil barraged Marlee with a daily flow of letters, and he must have composed them pretty effectively. For while Seth and Marlee got on well enough as long as Phil wasn't around, during the annual month that

Phil was back home he insinuated himself into Marlee's affections with an incredible ease.

Maybe it was inevitable, Phil being the physical idol of most girls' dreams. And he had an innate agressiveness that men like Seth, with a self-conscious shyness lurking behind an ardent front, could never honestly achieve.

Taken all in all, then, it wasn't too surprising that less than a week after Phil Umberhine's graduation from West Point—number five in his class of two hundred and ten—he and Marlee Benton were wed in a lavish ceremony at St. Augustine's Episcopal Church in Boston.

Seth Brightlaw, freshly graduated from Harvard, received an invitation to attend the wedding. He did so, concealing his inner feelings behind a frozen smile. But he departed early from the reception festivities afterward, going to a saloon down by the docks to get stinking drunk and spend the night with a couple of compliant floozies.

That was his initiation to sex. He remembered hardly anything about it, which was probably just as well. He spent the next day recovering from a monumental hangover.

The day after that he went to the nearest recruiting office and enlisted in the U. S. Cavalry. It was a totally impulsive act, one he committed without consulting his parents. He was immediately dispatched to Jefferson Barracks, Missouri, training ground for the Army of the West.

At the time it had seemed an easy out. Now, nearly three years later, Brightlaw felt nothing but a bitter regret. His act of silly and impulsive defiance had solved nothing. By now he hated the army, but he wouldn't abase his own pride by deserting, going on the run, being forced to change his identity. Nor did he want to face the possibility of a long prison term in Leavenworth if a federal marshal should catch up with him.

That left just one option: to sweat out his enlistment period and, once he was released, to take up the practice of law in a new life. He didn't care where. Any place that wasn't likely to arouse the rancid memories of youth. About two weeks of reading for the law should qualify him for the bench in any state or territory.

And now, by some cruel caprice, the past had come swarming back to haunt him. Coincidence? Sure. But a lot of stranger coincidences happened every day of a man's life. They just weren't as important.

Brightlaw only hoped that he could ride this one out. Phil Umberhine as his troop commander. And Marlee . . .

Bitter retrospections ran haphazardly through Seth Brightlaw's mind as he peered into the shaving mirror, whittling away a several days' growth of beard. He scowled at his image in the tarnished glass.

His gaunt and somber face, deeply browned by desert sun, looked older than his twenty-five years warranted. His thick shock of chestnut hair contrasted sharply with the pale gray of his eyes, and his long nose divided his face like a blade. It wasn't a bad-looking face for all that: men found it likable, and not a few women had found it attractive.

Brightlaw was of about average height and build, lean and wiry, lighter than most men his age. He had an easy grace about him and could move quickly. The tough seasoning of cavalry experience had left him in far better physical shape than he'd have been in if he had followed his father's urging to join his law office. The merciless grueling life of a cavalry trooper had its beneficial side. And a younger man could bear up well under it, even if the effects of yesterday's ordeal at the corral were still painfully kinking his muscles.

At the moment the long barracks building was deserted except for Brightlaw. He was standing in front of a mirror mounted on the west wall over a lone washstand. A man took his time shaving whenever he got a chance, especially when Sergeant Hanrahan was riding his ass at every opportunity.

Brightlaw finished up his shave, wiped traces of lather from his face, and pulled on his blouse. He was putting together his shaving kit when Trooper Pulvermacher came tramping into the barracks.

"Good morning, Seth!"

"Try to tell me what's good about it."

Max followed Brightlaw back to his bunk, then sprawled his broad bulk on his own bunk, which adjoined it, folding his arms behind his head. "Well, *mein freund*," he said placidly, "for one thing the good sergeant is not bearing down so hard on you. He is so mad about Lieutenant Umberhine."

Brightlaw nodded sourly. "Which does serve the sole advantage of keeping his attention off me."

"*Ja.*" Pulvermacher chuckled and shifted his weight, making the boards of his bunk groan in protest. "So why do you complain?"

"No reason. Just pitching pennies, I guess."

Brightlaw settled on the edge of his bunk, trying to look and sound more or less indifferent.

He was cautiously closemouthed by nature, as was Max. They had never confided much in one another, except to admit a common hatred for the army. Each was deliberately vague about his past, which was unusual for army buddies. But it was probably one reason they got along so well, together with the fact that each was unusually well educated. Max had dropped a couple of idle scholarly references to "Heidelberg" and "Vienna" before catching himself.

"Sarge is really set up about Umberhine, eh?"

"It's funny." Another gut-deep chuckle erupted from Max. "Hanrahan rides you because, it is said, he does not like Bostonians. But now Umberhine is troop commander and from Boston, too, and he is very tough, the grapevine has it. He will be giving Hanrahan all the orders!"

"Yeah," Brightlaw said moodily, rubbing his fresh-shaven chin. "Funny as hell."

"*Ja.*" Pulvermacher lifted his head. "You did not by chance know Umberhine back in Boston, Seth, did you?"

"Slightly," Brightlaw lied. "Our families knew each other. That was about it."

Pulvermacher eyed him shrewdly, seeming to sense that he'd stepped a bit over the line. Abruptly he rolled off his bunk and clapped Brightlaw on the shoulder. "Well, for stable duty we are about due, eh? That is what you and I are assigned next, the line sergeant tells me."

Brightlaw made a wry face, and Max laughed. "At least there will be no horse-breaking today. We just clean and curry horses. That will not be so bad . . . . ."

They left the barracks and angled across the parade ground toward the stables.

Across the quadrangle Sergeant Hanrahan was mercilessly grilling a dozen green recruits in a loud, angry voice. He seemed nearly to have forgotten any particular animus against Seth Brightlaw. The sergeant was more concerned with his overwhelming resentment of Umberhine, who, as Brightlaw knew, could be as insufferably arrogant as any man alive— as well as being Hanrahan's immediate superior.

Yet Brightlaw wondered what had originally implanted such an intense rage in Hanrahan. It seemed to range beyond all reason, beyond any normal resentment.

The buildings that flanked the big quadrangle were of mixed adobe and cottonwood-pole construction. For sanitary purposes the stables and latrines were built on a slight down-slant from both the officers' and enlisted men's barracks and the headquarters. At this early hour the post was already cooking under the sun—another predictable day on the Mojave Desert. No wonder Fort Burnshaw had a reputation for being the army's own special portal to Hell.

Brightlaw and Pulvermacher reported to the stable sergeant, a cherubic, easygoing man on the fifteenth year of his twenty-year enlistment.

Sergeant Gafke bunked in the stable and was responsible for seeing that all animals were properly cared for, as they were the key to any smooth-functioning cavalry unit. The horses spent each day outside. They were watered and fed at regular hours, groomed twice a day in garrison, and always on the picket line.

It was an easy detail, if a tedious one. A stable policeman was supposed to spend two hours grooming a horse above the knees, two hours currying him below. That was a typical stipulation of "The Book," any one of the miscellaneous manuals thrown together by some rump-sprung genius in Washington. If they'd followed it to the letter, troopers would have had no time at all for their many other activities. Nevertheless, all animals were immaculately tended, and there'd be hell to pay if they weren't.

Brightlaw and Pulvermacher were put to work on the picket line just beyond the stables, keeping methodically in tandem as they curried the horses side by side. They didn't hurry themselves or talk much. The sullen blanket of heat that dulled a man's faculties also discouraged much conversation or any effort at hard work.

Brightlaw paused to straighten up and ease a kink out of his back. Gazing idly across the parade ground, he began to massage his lower back with both hands. Then he froze in place.

Coming toward them across the quadrangle was Marlee Umberhine.

CHAPTER FOUR

O H CHRIST, BRIGHTLAW THOUGHT. HE HAD KNOWN THE meeting was bound to be, had inwardly braced himself for it, but couldn't help instinctively recoiling from the prospect.

Marlee halted a yard from him. "How are you, Seth?" she asked quietly.

She hadn't changed much in three years, unless to become even more strikingly beautiful. Her darkly auburn hair, caught up in shining coils atop her head, caught glints of sun-blaze. Her face was a study in exotic slants and tilts, with its high cheekbones and somewhat long but straight aristocratic nose. Her full lips were tucked together almost primly, unsmiling. She was tall, close to his height, and her costly green riding habit set off her trim figure and matched her eyes, as did the small tricorne perched on her head.

"Right as rain, thank you, Miz Umberhine."

Brightlaw was a fairly accomplished mime. He spoke tonelessly, in the twangy drawl of the Southwest, aware that Pulvermacher had straightened up in astonishment and was staring at them. *Damn!* His past was bound to leak out now . . . although he could caution Max, at least, to silence.

The faint trace of a smile lifted the corners of her mouth. "I used to be worth more than a 'Miz Umberhine,' Seth."

"That was a spell back."

"Yes, wasn't it?" She gave Max Pulvermacher a full and dazzling smile now. "Please don't let me interrupt your work, Trooper."

Max's face went as red as a beet as he returned to furiously brushing one of the horses.

Brightlaw didn't know what to say. He felt like an idiot with ten thumbs. At the same time he was cruelly aware of the fierce longing he'd always felt whenever Marlee was close. But he couldn't have guessed it would wrench at him this strongly. Or that she could seem more alluring, more desirable, than ever.

His fist clenched so tightly around the curry brush that his knuckles ached.

Marlee glanced at the brush and said smilingly, "Would you lay that down a moment, Seth? I would like to go for a ride, and I thought you might choose me a likely mount."

"We do not keep ladies' saddles in stock," Brightlaw said stiffly.

"I shouldn't think so." Marlee tapped her riding quirt lightly against one palm. "But Mrs. Traviston, the commandant's wife, has a sidesaddle, and she has granted me the use of it, if I wish. Would you . . . ?"

Setting his jaw like a trap, Brightlaw laid down the curry brush and led the way into the ammoniac-smelling stable.

The long building was well lighted, for each horse had its own stall with a window venting on it; each had a manger and clean straw bedding on an earth floor. Saddles were hung on strong supporting pins along the heel post of each stall, and the bridles were mounted on smaller pins. Each stall that housed an officer's favorite mount had a pasteboard sign mounted above it, inscribed with the horse's name and the officer's as well.

Brightlaw tramped clear to the end of the stable and lifted down Mrs. Traviston's sidesaddle. "This is the one you want, ma'am. Miz Traviston's mare is out on the picket line, and she is a gentle beast. I recommend that you borrow her for your ride, if Miz Traviston would be willing."

"She would be." Marlee's green gaze was fixed on his face, and he wished to God he was anywhere but here. "Seth . . . let's have an end to this travesty. Can't we speak frankly? There was a time when we could."

Brightlaw's impersonal tone turned low and hard. "We said it all back then."

"But it was a long time ago! Seth . . ."

"Three years."

"That," Marlee said bitterly, "might just be a lifetime, for some."

Brightlaw didn't reply; he only watched her curiously. What did she mean? Knowing Phil Umberhine, though, he could already guess.

"It's been hell, Seth," she said in a low, passionate voice. "He's a devil. Or the closest thing to one in human guise. I had no idea, believe me. If I told you of all the indignities, the *obscenities*, he has inflicted on—"

"I don't want to hear it," Brightlaw broke in harshly. "Listen, Marlee . . . it's over. It's done with. I've gone through enough on that account."

She studied his face for a long moment, then whispered, "You knew he was like that, didn't you? How hateful he could be."

"Yes."

"And you never said a word!"

Brightlaw let his shoulders lift and fall in a small, weary shrug. "You wouldn't have listened."

"No." Marlee shut her eyes tightly. "That's true. I'm not blaming you. I just wish . . ." She bit her underlip and opened her eyes. "Do you hear from home, ever? From your folks?"

"We keep in touch."

"But you never went back to Boston . . . after joining up."

"Wasn't much chance. If you're posted way out here and you get a furlough, you go to the nearest city or town or 'hog ranch' or whatever, and spend it there. Your leaves aren't long enough that you can afford to spend the whole time traveling home and back."

Brightlaw's tone was almost indifferent, but he watched her face, trying to read whatever lay behind it. She seemed very cool and collected again, and a small crooked smile touched one corner of her mouth.

"Those furloughs . . . I suppose most of them are spent roistering about."

"You might call it that." Brightlaw kept his voice flat and neutral. "A trooper goes as his fellows go. Most of it would be unfit for a lady's ears. But you've been married into the army long enough to know that."

"Yes." She let out a soft and ragged sigh. "Haven't I just."

How simple it was to reduce everything that had been to a lot of trivial prattle. But what else was there to say, after all?

A shadow crossed the packed-dirt floor of the stable runway. Lieutenant Philip Umberhine was standing in the archway, his teeth bared in that enormously genial grin.

"Hello, my dear. Managed to get all that paperwork out of the way sooner than I expected, so I thought I would join you on your ride. Good morning, Seth."

"Good morning, sir."

Brightlaw swiveled on his heel to face Umberhine, snapping a crisp salute. Umberhine acknowledged it with an idle flip of his right hand at his hat brim as he moved forward, casually taking Marlee by one arm. She didn't quite wince, but seeing her lips compress tightly, Brightlaw knew that Umberhine was applying a cruel degree of pressure with his grip.

"Well, well," Umberhine said, smiling, "It must be pleasant for you two to stand about making memories. Really hate to break it up."

Brightlaw kept his face very still and bland, and he said nothing.

Phil Umberhine was a large man. He topped Seth by several inches and he was heavily built, broad and beefy. His looping black mustaches tended to narrow a square and blocky face that was nearly as handsome as it had been a few years ago. Though Phil was now somewhat overweight, Brightlaw thought he looked solid enough. His dark eyes sparkled with a contempt that his open and friendly smile couldn't disguise.

Phil used to kick the shit out of him regularly, Brightlaw remembered. He could likely do as much now. But he wouldn't need to. Phil had the authority to make a subordinate suffer in any way he chose . . . and never lay a hand on him personally.

Brightlaw thought: *He'll do it, too.*

Although Seth's expression was calm, he had a wild desire to strike out at this brass-flaunting bastard. The tendril of an idea edged wickedly into his mind.

I'll pay for it later, Brightlaw thought. But he'll make me pay no matter what. So what's to lose?

"I was about to saddle a horse for Mrs. Umberhine. I can saddle one for you too, sir."

Umberhine nodded amiably. "I was about to order you to. Do it."

"Yes, sir. Any particular saddle?"

Umberhine pointed a thumb at the saddle that hung under Colonel Traviston's name. He did it with his usual casual arrogance, and Brightlaw had to suppress a smile. Same old Phil.

He went to the picket line and singled out Mrs. Traviston's favorite horse for Marlee, cinched on the sidesaddle, then handed the reins to Marlee.

"I'll help you to mount up in a few moments, ma'am."

"Would you, Seth? Thanks."

Her voice held only a faint trace of irony, and again Brightlaw had to check a smile. He tramped back into the stable, lifted down Traviston's saddle, carried it out to the picket line, and slung it across the back of Old Bloody Bay.

When the big blood bay was readied, he led him to Umberhine and handed him the reins, then went back to Marlee. But he didn't at once hand her up to the saddle. Brightlaw halted beside her, then turned to watch Umberhine swing his bulk aboard the blood bay.

The results were everything that Brightlaw could have hoped for.

Old Bloody Bay had stood as tranquil as a statue up till that moment. Then he exploded into action.

He went into his pile-driving routine at once, almost dislodging Umberhine on the first leap. The lieutenant was caught wholly off guard. He nearly lost his seat but then held on gamely, teeth gritted, as the blood bay went through his usual procedure of wild pitchings. From his own experience with the animal Brightlaw could predict each of the animal's follow-up moves.

Now came the sudden switch to sunfishing. It almost threw Phil off, but he was a skilled horseman. He shifted his weight in time and managed to shift it again as the horse changed leads.

Then the blood bay went back to sunfishing. Umberhine was jolted savagely from one side to the other, and his face was ruddy with rage. He sent Brightlaw a single venomous glance, but that was all he had time for.

Old Bloody Bay was lunging away toward the breaking corral, with every intention of smashing side-on against the fence and crushing his rider's leg.

Umberhine barely sensed the animal's strategy in time. "Jesus Christ!" he yelled, and flung himself sideways out of the saddle.

He hit the ground heavily. He rolled over and over from the sheer impetus of his fall and came to a stop facedown in the dust, where he lay panting and coughing, too stunned to get up very quickly.

Old Bloody Bay came to a halt and stood placidly now, as Brightlaw went over to pick up his trailing reins. Briefly he met Marlee's glance, and she was making no move toward Phil. It was Seth whom she watched, and she held one hand clasped over her mouth.

Brightlaw suspected that it covered a smile.

Umberhine heaved himself slowly and painfully to his feet, shaking his head. Batting dust from his blouse and trousers, he walked slowly over to Brightlaw. He stood swaying a little, still unsteady on his feet. Max Pulvermacher was staring at them, open-mouthed.

"You did that deliberately, didn't you?" Umberhine said huskily. "That damned nag was all primed to do what he did. *And you knew it!*"

"I'm afraid I don't know what you mean, sir."

"Like so much shit, you don't." Umberhine spoke calmly, studying Brightlaw's face. He'd like to take a swing at me here and now, Brightlaw thought.

He was braced for something of the sort. Surprisingly, Umberhine only smiled. "You've bought it now, Seth," he said gently. "You've brought yourself more trouble than any man needs."

"Afraid I still don't know what you mean, sir," Brightlaw said, poker-faced.

"Well, perhaps I can enlighten you. Regulations forbid me to brawl on the fort grounds. I wouldn't care to break the rules and I'm sure you wouldn't. Am I correct?"

"Yes, sir."

"Do you know of a place off the military reservation where we might settle the matter in private?"

"I believe so, sir," Brightlaw said promptly. "Henry Chance's barn is off the post."

"Fine . . . fine." Umberhine bared his teeth again, not pleasantly. "You name the time, Trooper. I'll be there."

CHAPTER FIVE

Brightlaw was lighting a lantern hung from a nail driven into a small post when he heard the footsteps approaching Chance's barn. Quickly he crossed the runway to the opposite stall and shrank against the boards, waiting.

He had taken the precaution of asking Henry Chance, who also served as post sutler, if it would be okay for him and a member of the troop (left unnamed by Brightlaw) to settle a difference of opinion in his barn after reveille that evening. Chance had amiably agreed. Wasn't much damage a pair of brawlers could inflict inside a spacious barn. He'd turn the horses and mules out to his corral before retiring.

One of the two doors at the end of the stable runway swung open on nicely oiled hinges. A bulky figure loomed in the lamplight against the graying darkness outside.

"Push it shut, Phil," Brightlaw said. "And be quick about it, if you please."

Umberhine hesitated, resenting the disrespectful command. But he conceded by hauling the door shut, to lock in the lamplight and whatever went on inside.

Brightlaw had already shoved a buggy against the closed opposite doors of the runway, and now he said mildly, "Mind helping me drag a buggy against these other doors, too? It'll discourage anyone from barging in on us suddenly."

Umberhine nodded, and the two of them laid hold of another buggy and rolled it solidly against the twin doors. Then Umberhine unfastened his pistol belt and tossed it on the buggy seat, afterward removing his hat and peeling off his blouse. Brightlaw did the same, and the two of them moved wordlessly out to the scuffed clay floor of the runway and cautiously squared off.

Brightlaw saw the stir of great muscles beneath Umberhine's undershirt. He had the bleak conviction, once again, that it would likely be another repetition of their boyhood quarrels. Back then, Phil had beaten up on him with contemptuous ease. He had a couple years on Seth, of course, but mostly he'd had overwhelming size and weight, even then. Now he was a lot bigger, and he wore the same insufferably arrogant look that said, "I can smash you or any insect like you."

But Seth was full-grown himself now, and he was as trim and hard as a board. Phil was still solid-looking, but he had taken on quite a bit of girth, an indication that he hadn't bothered to keep himself in very good shape these last few years. Probably he'd been stationed at some desk job somewhere east of Jefferson Barracks, with little occasion or inclination to exert himself.

Brightlaw noted these things and felt a fleeting lift of hope. *By God, maybe I can do it.* More likely not, but at least he might leave some marks on the bastard. Even that much would make it worthwhile. And thinking back now, he could feel a gathering of long-stored wrath in him, the kind that made a man want to smash out and kill.

He was amused by the way Umberhine cocked his fists in the traditional style of John L. Sullivan. And he realized that an involuntary smile had begun to shape itself on his lips.

"Think it's funny, Seth?" Umberhine whistled between his teeth. "Tell me how funny *this* is."

He barged in hugely, swinging with both fists. Brightlaw danced quickly and easily out of reach. Then in the manner of a man who had endured too many bruising fights fought under Marquis of Queensbury rules in his time, he wheeled suddenly around behind Umberhine.

With both fists knotted tightly together he slammed them into Phil's kidneys. Umberhine's body arched backward; an explosive grunt left him. Then he pitched forward on the clay floor, his arms outflung.

I could stomp his ass right now, Brightlaw thought wickedly, then smiled again and stepped back. In a barroom brawl a man might resort to any tactics. But they were *gentlemen*, he and Phil. They were supposed to comport themselves (at least in theory) as gentlemen should.

Umberhine rolled over on his back, groaning, and the front of his immaculate underwear was plastered with wet clay. He rubbed a hand across it and stared at the hand. A mingled look of disbelief and chagrin checkered his expression.

"Why . . ." he murmured, "you bastard. You slimy little bastard."

"No rules on this ground, Phil," Brightlaw said quietly. "You wore all the polish off the rules a long time ago. Years ago."

A naked fury lit Umberhine's face now. He rolled upward on his haunches and came driving at Brightlaw in a savage lunge, pistoning himself forward almost before he was wholly on his feet.

Brightlaw moved quickly sideways, but not fast enough. One of Phil's burly outflung arms caught him around the legs and held on tight as they both crashed to the floor. Umberhine tried to roll atop him and pin him by sheer weight and power, but Brightlaw's roughshod saloon brawling stood him in good stead again.

Before Umberhine could position himself, Seth drove a knee savagely into his groin. Umberhine's face contorted with anguish. He rolled limply away, clutching himself.

Brightlaw scrambled quickly to his feet and once more stood off, breathing a little heavily now, waiting till the lieutenant was able to recover enough to stagger to his feet.

But this time there was a killing hatred in Umberhine's face. And now, aware of what he was up against, he would be more careful. A twisted caution marked his face, without dimming the crazed lust of his rage.

"You wanted this pretty goddamned bad, Seth, didn't you?"

Brightlaw shook his head gently. "I never wanted it. I admired you once. A long time back. And you used me for a football. You'd do it all over again. Only it won't be that easy."

"That's what you think," Umberhine whispered, "you crummy little turd. Watch yourself."

He came circling in, sparring lightly, feinting and parrying at Brightlaw. Seth simply kept backing away, watching Umberhine with caution, taking care not to let himself get maneuvered against a wall or into a corner. If Umberhine got him cornered, he could still pummel the crap out of him without much difficulty.

Hoping to divert his attention a little, Brightlaw said, "Phil, you haven't treated Marlee too well, she tells me."

"Is that right?" Umberhine grinned wickedly. He feinted swiftly at Brightlaw's face. "She told you that, did she?"

"I just said it."

"Yeah?" Umberhine faked a rushing motion, and Brightlaw stepped easily out of the way, still keeping in the open. "What else did she tell you?"

"Not much. But I sort of wondered—" Brightlaw danced quickly sideways, out of the path of Umberhine's next savage swing.

"Wondered what?"

"I wondered if you came to the stable hoping to catch us together. Talking was all we did. But you wanted to catch us together."

"Why, yes." Umberhine grinned. "Of course I did. Why else do you think I'd do it?"

Brightlaw felt a bitter flare of anger now. He lunged forward far enough to take a direct swing at Umberhine's face.

The lieutenant leaped back, barely evading Brightlaw's fist. Then he took a long step forward and tried to connect with Brightlaw's jaw. His swing missed, but Brightlaw had to move backward so quickly that his shoulder banged against the lantern suspended on a stall post.

Light and shadow danced crazily. It threw every object in the barn into confusion. In that moment Umberhine rushed

Brightlaw, seized hold of him bodily, and then flung him with all his considerable strength into one of the stalls.

Brightlaw struck the far wall with an impact that drove the breath from him. Then Umberhine was advancing into the stall, his big arms spread sideways. Brightlaw was trapped inside the stall. If Umberhine ever got those powerful arms around him . . .

Brightlaw was pinned against the wall. But behind him, suspended from a nail, was a tangle of strap leather. It was composed of the odds and ends that any harnessmaker was likely to leave hanging about.

Just as Umberhine was almost on him Brightlaw reached back and upward, ripped the tangle of dangling leather from the wall, and hurled it at Phil's head.

Umberhine gave a startled bawl of rage. He fell backward a couple of steps. He was still trying to tear the tangled mess of leather from his head when Brightlaw moved in on him, half crouching, to pound quick solid blows into Phil's midriff and force him to stumble backward out of the stall.

Now Brightlaw was in the open again.

He resumed his slow, circling motion as Umberhine tore the tangle of harness from his head and flung it to the stable floor. He wore a crazed and savage look, and he was far from finished.

"I'm going to kill you, Seth," he whispered.

Instead of going after Brightlaw bare-fisted again, Umberhine wheeled and strode to a pitchfork leaning against a stall post. Quick as thought he whipped it up and turned, hurling it at Brightlaw as a man might throw a spear.

Brightlaw threw himself to the dank stable floor barely in time. The pitchfork passed inches above him; he heard it boom hollowly into the stable wall.

He tried to roll out of the way as Umberhine ran toward him and viciously swung a booted foot at his head. He only partly succeeded. The boot scraped along Brightlaw's head and sent his senses reeling.

But the strength of desperation fed Brightlaw's muscles.

The boot was still there, close to his head. He seized hold of it and twisted, hard.

Already off balance, Umberhine was turned in mid-stride. He crashed on his side and lay momentarily stunned.

Brightlaw floundered forward on his hands and knees. Then his legs gave out and he landed flat on the stable floor by Umberhine. He still had enough energy left to drive several sledging, savage blows into Phil's face.

Umberhine was able to recover sufficiently to thrust Brightlaw away from him. Seth lit on his back and then was able to roll over enough to face Umberhine.

Both men were spent. They lay only a couple of feet from each other, their nostrils full of the reeking barn floor, but both were too exhausted to continue the fray.

"God damn you, Seth," Umberhine said tiredly.

"Same to you."

"All right. We've had our fracas. It didn't prove anything worth a good goddamn." Umberhine lay on his side, his breath coming in heavy gulps. "But you mark this, Seth. I told you before to watch it. Now you'll have a real reason for believing me. Because I'm going to hang your ass out to cure and dry. Only you won't die fast. You'll just die a hell of a lot slower. And that'll make it more than worth it. . . ."

CHAPTER SIX

THERE WERE A LOT OF THINGS THAT A TROOP COMMANDER could do to make his troopers' lives a living hell. If the commander held a grudge against a particular trooper, persecution could be raised to a fine art.

The types of brutal punishment inflicted on enlisted men were derived from an older day. They had been carried on through the Civil War and still prevailed in the frontier cavalry. It was a time of hard drinking, and after payday half of a garrison might become so drunk and disorderly as to invite official action. A drunk might be bound, then gagged with a bar of yellow army soap for a few hours. Or he might be spread-eagled on a wagon wheel for a day, with the bulging hub of the wheel crunched into his back. Or, if caught staggering about with his bottle, he would be given the task of burying it. This consisted of digging a hole ten feet square by ten feet deep, reverently laying the bottle to rest in it, and then filling in the hole again. All great ways to sweat out the hooch.

Unfortunately for Umberhine, Trooper Brightlaw's behavior (at least while he was on the post) was so exemplary that the lieutenant had to forgo the pleasure of inflicting any unusual punishment. He merely saw to it that if there was any particularly obnoxious detail to which a man could be assigned, Brightlaw was to be on it.

Actually, although their professed duty was to defend the frontier, few of any company's personnel were likely to be on the warpath at any given time. Most of the time, by far, they were assigned to any number of petty jobs. These could range from planting and harvesting gardens, building roads or bridges, quarrying stone, burning brick and lime, driving teams, making hay, herding cattle, sawing planks, and constructing stables and barracks, to cultivating a flower plot for the CO's wife. Brightlaw would barely finish one duty before he was assigned to another.

Both Max Pulvermacher and Idaho Bitters were concerned about their friend. Brightlaw was becoming more gaunt and worn-down with every passing day. Sometimes it was all he could manage just to stagger out of his bunk to serve on another grueling detail.

"You can register a complaint with the commandant!" Pulvermacher declared, vehemently. "It is your right, Seth. And we've seen what it's doing to you. We can testify to it!"

"That's right," Idaho Bitters drawled. "It's been goin' on for a month now. We can both back up anything that comes out about that son of a bitch. You just say the word, Seth."

Brightlaw only smiled and shook his head.

It would be hard to explain to either man why he wouldn't, or couldn't, follow the advice. Privately, he guessed that it narrowed down to two reasons. First, there was the matter of a man's own pride and personal dignity. He was double-damned if he was going to let Umberhine, or any man, break him down to a sniveling complainer. Second, any revelation about what had led to this situation would mean the baring of an unpleasant past, and that would hurt Marlee.

Damned if he'd do that.

But Brightlaw was fetched a real surprise when, on a late evening while he was posted on sentry duty along the fort's perimeter, carrying his rifle drag-fisted and feeling so weary that he thought he might collapse at any moment, he was approached by Sergeant Michael Hanrahan.

He first saw a man's form sidling toward him through the darkness, and was about to throw up his rifle and yell, "Halt! Who goes there?" when he recognized Hanrahan's broad, shambling form. Nobody else looked or walked like that.

He stopped in his tracks, waiting in place till Hanrahan

came up to him and halted. The sergeant took out a stogie and lit it, shaking a sulphurous flare of sparks from the match. The glow dimly illuminated his stolid, rough-hewn face.

"Pardon me, Trooper," he said mildly. "I'd offer ye a smoke, but I believe you don't indulge."

"No I don't, Sarge. But thanks for the good thought."

Brightlaw's tone was only slightly sarcastic. He wondered why the hell Hanrahan, who had ridden his ass so viciously for so long, was now taking an amiable tack with him.

"It's like this," Hanrahan continued in the same mild voice. "I've hated your guts because you're from Boston. From the same class that's put my people through misery."

"I never did," Brightlaw said flatly. "Never me as an individual, I mean."

"Aye. I understand that now." Hanrahan's face showed a tight frown as he puffed rapidly on his cigar, each inhalation causing the live coal to light up his face. "It's that bastard troop commander of ours. I've watched the way he's come down on you this past month. I've never seen such ill-treatment of a man. It's worse than any I ever done on you."

Brightlaw said dryly, "Even fellow Bostonians from the same class can hate each other."

"Aye." Hanrahan rubbed a hand over his beard, embarrassedly. "What I'm saying, bucko, is that I realize it ain't the nationality. It's the man. Umberhine has it in for you, and while I'm not the man to ask why, I now realize that, coming from the same class as ye both do, there can still be a mighty hatred between the twain. Do ye see my meaning?"

"I reckon I do, Sarge."

"All right, then." Hanrahan pulled the stogie from his jaws, threw it down, and ground it underfoot. "Umberhine had also been wicked as hell toward us Irish troopers. Toward all the others also, but toward us in particular."

"I've noticed."

"Well, then." Hanrahan lowered his voice almost to a whisper. "Would you care to join a bunch of us who plan to desert? Just get out of this fucking army?"

Brightlaw wasn't very surprised at the proposal. The desertion rate in the Army of the West was overwhelming, and most of any company regiment was made up of Irishmen.

"I can't do that, Sarge," he said slowly. "I appreciate the offer, but I just can't do it. Doesn't have anything to do with glory or honor, anything like that. It's just me."

Hanrahan leaned a little forward, as if trying to make out Brightlaw's expression in the dim sheen of moonlight. Then he chuckled softly.

"Aye. I grasp your meanin'. But you'd be welcome to join us if ye should have a mind to. I can even offer you a time and place to desert."

"I'd rather you didn't," Brightlaw said quietly. "If you intend to do it, fine. If you should foul up, your friends might blame me for giving you away. I wouldn't want anything like that."

Hanrahan guffawed loudly. "Aye! You're a gentleman bred to the bone. And I mean that in the finest way, Sassenach. But watch yourself. Our bastard of a troop commander is not done with ye. . . ."

In theory no doubt Hanrahan was right, but as it turned out Brightlaw had less than one more day to suffer under the lieutenant's cruel mistreatment.

Early the next morning Colonel Traviston announced that the Mojave Indians, in a sudden uprising, had been conducting raids against the settlers near San Bernardino. B Troop was to be turned out in full force to put down the uprising.

Lieutenant Umberhine lost no time in assembling his company. These were men riding out to war, and they prepared for it with a grim efficiency. The call "To Horse" echoed across the post. B Troop was formed on the parade ground and roll was taken. Umberhine, reins dangling from one hand, stood a little apart with other officers. Hanrahan and the other sergeants reported a head count to the officers, who in turn reported to Umberhine, and the order to mount was given.

B Troop passed out through the west sentry gate in columns of two, their guidons barely stirring in the warm, still morning. They angled right, past the corner of the sutler's post. A couple of dogs, feeling lively for the short period of time before the hot sun would drive them to shade, romped across the parade ahead of the men, barking wildly.

As they passed the officers' quarters, Brightlaw glanced sideways. Marlee Umberhine stood in a doorway, one shoulder leaning against the jamb. She was wearing a gray wrapper, and her arms were casually folded.

But her eyes followed him, nobody else.

Too late, Brightlaw thought. Too long ago and too late now, Marlee.

He held his face stiff and still as they rode out of the fort. But he felt Max Pulvermacher's watchful gaze on him. Pulvermacher was riding next to him.

And just ahead of them, First Sergeant Hanrahan was jogging along. You didn't have to guess when Hanrahan intended to desert. The jaunty set of his thick shoulders said it all.

He intended to break out of the army, and it would be damned soon.

CHAPTER SEVEN

THE DAY'S HEAT HAD ALREADY TURNED FIERCE AS AN OVEN about an hour after B Troop rode out from Fort Burnshaw. Their troop strength was twenty-three men, unusually large for any contingent posted on the Mojave.

The sun shortly baked away whatever enthusiastic vinegar they'd started out with, as they tackled the route south of Vegas Springs that late-arriving settlers were now designating as Las Vegas. They were on the government road, if you could call it a road, that would take them to San Bernardino. It was no more than a pair of shallow wagon ruts that would guide freighters and stage drivers to their destination. This, in fact, was the main reason that the U.S Army maintained troops in the Mojave at all: to protect freight wagons and stagecoaches against any Indian threat.

It was after sundown when Lieutenant Umberhine called a halt at a murky thread of stream that barely flowed at all. The last ruddy rays of the sun were dissolving into twilight. The troopers felt fried, half-dead, as they piled groaning off their mounts. They had to walk and water the animals, then tether them to a picket line and grain them, before they were permitted to build fires against the coming dusk.

It took the murderous heat of a high-summer day in the Mojave Desert to make the trooper on trek realize just how relatively cushy an existence he'd actually enjoyed on the post. At first it had seemed a relief to escape the tedium of cutting hay, tending animals, improving the post grounds, going through ordinary drills, and so on. But no longer.

As he, Brightlaw, and Pulvermacher wearily prepared their supper rations over a brush fire, Idaho Bitters drawled, "Jee-zus. You reckon it always gets this hot when a man's on the move?"

"Hotter," Max Pulvermacher said promptly. "This is not so bad, my friend. Sometimes on the Mojave it goes way above one hundred and twenty-five degrees on Dr. Fahrenheit's scale."

Idaho smiled crookedly. "How'n hell does a foreigner like you know all that, Dutchy?"

"I do not mean to sound ponderous. But always I read. I study. And most of all, I just keep my ears open. I listen. Sometime you ought to try it, my friend, eh?"

"Max is a real scholar." Brightlaw grinned out of the fog of his own tiredness. "You pick up a lot of things that way, old pal."

Idaho only snorted and reached over to touch the coffeepot he'd set by the fire. It hadn't yet begun to boil, but he yanked his hand back from the hot metal, swearing mildly.

The three men were hunkered down by their fire. Other beacons of flame pierced the growing dusk around them. The silence of the desert was punctuated by the murmurs of the troopers.

Brightlaw's gaze ranged off to his far right, studying First Lieutenant Umberhine and First Sergeant Hanrahan. The two of them were standing on a rise of ground at a little distance, darkly outlined against the graying horizon. Their voices, if not their words, reached faintly across the encampment.

Nobody else seemed to be interested. The troopers were too tired and sour to care much, especially since Umberhine and Hanrahan had clashed from the first, and they all knew it. Umberhine's manner was the same with everyone: outwardly bland and amused but inwardly inexorable. He could afford to be any of these, since he was the ultimate authority here. He'd patiently hear out Hanrahan's choppy, strident, frustrated bitchings, then simply ignore them.

Abruptly Hanrahan turned and wheeled away down the

rise, tense with fury as he joined a pair of his Irish compatriots at their fire.

Umberhine was brewing up a pot of trouble for himself and the troop, Brightlaw reflected. But Hanrahan could be just as bullheaded and arrogant as his troop commander, and nothing good would come of it. This was an understaffed outfit on what might prove to be a harrowing mission.

According to the post grapevine, which you could believe about half the time, Umberhine had insisted to Colonel Traviston that his troop alone could quash any force of undisciplined savages they came up against. Maybe they could, after a fashion.

Like the Apaches, the Mojave warriors tended to commit their depredations in small bands, rarely more than a dozen warriors apiece. But having inherited all the desert savvy of their forebears, they could be damned effective on their own ground. They'd make swift guerilla-like forays, always hitting by surprise. If they saw that odds were against them, they would fall into swift retreat, fading out of sight in the trackless desert. Nearly always, a desert-bred fighter would survive to fight another day.

Among the commisioned officers of the frontier army, only General George Crook seemed to have a practical awareness of that fact. When pursuing marauding Indians, Crook adopted their own tactics, using provision-laden packhorses (rather than wagons) to follow them into their nearly impassable strongholds. But nobody of Crook's caliber was in charge of this far-flung region.

All they could count on here was the likes of Colonel Traviston, or worse yet, a green and pompous ass like Umberhine. Phil was smart enough; he simply couldn't see past the end of his own complacent nose. Nothing but experience could season him. If he lived that long . . .

Max and Idaho had both taken note of Brightlaw's straying attention.

"What you reckon them shamrocks are yammering about?" Idaho said. "Hanrahan looks pretty pissed."

"What is that?" Pulvermacher asked. "This means uri-nated?"

"It's a purely American term, Max," Brightlaw said gravely. "Means the Irish aren't too pleased with the lieutenant's authority."

Idaho jerked out a chuckle. "Neither's any of us, that I been able to tell."

"Nein." Pulvermacher nodded his head, slowly. "But these more so than others, I think."

"They're all full-blooded Irish," Brightlaw said. "If you didn't know, those other two guys—Coyne, he's the short fellow, and O'Flynn, he's the long bean pole of a man—are Irish immigrants like our sterling first sergeant. They've all been pushed into the same corner."

Both his comrades nodded in agreement at the same time. They understood that sort of situation.

Brightlaw thought fleetingly of Marlee. God—how much more would she have to endure at the hands of a self-serving bastard like Phil Umberhine? *And what the hell can you do about it in any case?*

"It is too bad," Pulvermacher said soberly. "It will divide the command, and that is no good. What will then happen, Seth?"

Brightlaw shook his head. "No way of telling for sure. Except that, whatever it is, it won't happen."

"But why is that?"

"Sarge and his buddies are aiming to desert. It'll come soon. You can bet on it."

Pulvermacher frowned. "But if you think so, should you not warn the lieutenant, Seth?"

"Shit," Idaho Bitters said softly. "That brass-head bastard won't listen. He already knows it all. Thinks he does anyway."

Brightlaw scrubbed a hand tiredly over his unshaven jaw. "That's about it, Max. He'll go any other way from anything I tell him, just because I told him."

Also, he had to silently admit, he was far from being out

of sympathy with Sergeant Michael Hanrahan and his cro-
nies. . . .

Brightlaw came upright in his blankets as the company
trumpeter blasted away the last shreds of sleep. Brightlaw
had scooped out a hollow for his hips in the ground, but he
still felt a quota of aches from a night of sleeping on the bare,
stony earth.

Pulvermacher and Idaho were rolling out, too. So were
others of the still weary troop. Just about all of them were
grumbling and quietly bitching. It wasn't yet time to be on
the march. The first crimson flush of dawn was coming up
sunlessly, making a silhouette, like a child's ragged cutout
from black paper, of the mountain range to the east.

"*Mein Gott,*" groaned Pulvermacher, shaking the sand
out of his blankets. "Why is it this early he is rousting out?
That was not enough sleep, so tired we were. What good
will we be for fighting?"

"He smells glory." Brightlaw grimaced as he massaged
his sore back with his palms. "He's hungry for a taste of
combat. He's never had any. No glory in peacetime for a
military soul."

"*Mein Gott,*" Pulvermacher muttered. "Even in America. This is what I left Bavaria for?"

"Them guys is the same any place you go, Dutchy," Idaho
said dourly as he rolled up his blankets. "Call it patriotism.
All right in its place, I reckon. But a lot of these brass-head
sombitches are just out for blood-letting. They get that much,
they don't care who gets hurt. The enemy, or just a passel of
peaceable folks who get in the way."

Brightlaw nodded. Idaho Bitters had been in the service
somewhat longer than either he or Max. "In our class," he
observed wryly, "Umberhine's and mine, citation and ad-
vancement were always big incentives. They're a large part
of it."

"Yeah," growled Idaho, "and it's the little guy that always takes it on the chin, be he soldier or reg'lar civilian.
Well, gentlemen, you figure we'll be allowed time to mash

up some hardtack and boil it up with beans for our breakfast, ha ha?''

Their night fire had died to cold ashes, and Max scoured up brush to replenish it while Brighlaw and Idaho broke up several chunks of hardtack.

Army hardtack must have been the inspiration of some demented genius who loathed military people. It was a plain flour-and-water biscuit formed in a flat rectangle roughly three inches long, two inches wide, and a half inch thick. It was so hard you needed a rock or your gun butt to bust it up. Or you might soak it to a soft consistency which, after a long period, would resemble a rubbery substance that some people could actually stomach. The troopers called it ''flour tile'' and usually pounded it into crumbs, then dumped it into soup or meat fat or even into the coffeepot. The last was a culinary hybrid that was inevitably called ''hardtack and coffee.'' If you could keep it down it might even sustain you awhile, depending on how hungry you were.

Fortunately, Brightlaw and his comrades had some left-over beans from supper last night, and could stretch them into a full meal with the aid of crumbled hardtack. After heating the mess together, they sat gagging it down.

While they were still eating, Line Sergeant Menzies came shambling up.

He was a middle-sized man, whose weather-troughed face was so dyspeptic and mournful that it was obvious that only long tenure in the ranks had advanced him to a first sergeant's status. In fact Barney Menzies was now the only sergeant in their troop, after Hanrahan. For God-knew-what official reason or other, no corporals had been available for this patrol. Just a lot of privates, all of them pretty green troopers at that.

''Morning, fellas,'' said Menzies.

Squatting on their heels, each of them gave him a polite nod, and then Brightlaw said: ''What's up, Barney? I take it this isn't a social call.''

''I reckon not, Seth. The lieutenant is pretty het up. Wants to see you right away.''

Brightlaw raised his brows. ''Oh? What about?''

"I dunno, 'cept that Sarge Hanrahan and a couple of his buddies deserted last night. We took a head count of the troop and they're the only ones missing."

Brightlaw sighed, glanced down at the almost inedible concoction on his plate, then laid it aside. He stood up, rubbing his back with both hands, still grimacing. "All right. Just me?"

Menzies nodded morosely. "I didn't hear him mention nobody else. I hazard he wants to talk with you private."

"What does that have to do with those deserters?"

"You best ask him, Seth," Menzies answered with the neutral caution of an old soldier. "He didn't tell me nothing else."

Brightlaw followed Menzies up a shallow rise and down its other side, where Lieutenant Phil Umberhine was enjoying a comfortable breakfast. His striker, a rather effeminate sort not dissimilar to Colonel Traviston's Sparling, had dished up a good meal of fresh biscuits, savory bacon, and fresh-brewed coffee.

Phil was seated cross-legged, leisurely eating, on the other side of the fire from Wolf Call, one of the scouts assigned to their command.

Umberhine glanced up as Brightlaw approached. "Ah, Trooper." He motioned at the bubbling coffeepot beside the fire. "Care for a cup?"

Brightlaw tried to ignore the tempting smell of *fresh* coffee—not the Santos coffee the regular troopers had to consume, which tasted like a cross between quinine and charred sawdust.

Brightlaw shook his head. "No, sir." He came to a halt and saluted smartly. "Thank you."

Umberhine merely tapped the brim of his hat with a finger and didn't bother to rise. He swigged his cup empty, took his time refilling it, then looked up at Brightlaw, squinting a little against the sharp beams of the rising sun.

"You know that our first sergeant has deserted the command?"

"I've been told, sir."

"Yes . . . Ah, dismissed, Menzies. You too, Adams."

Umberhine waved a hand, and Sergeant Menzies and the striker each saluted then tramped away across the rise.

Umberhine stared hard at Brightlaw. His gaze was like ice, chill and brittle. "What do you know about it, Seth?"

"Pardon, sir?"

"You know damned well what I mean. The desertion of three men. Michael Hanrahan, Daniel Coyne, Patrick O'Flynn. They slipped out of camp past our sentries last night. I don't know how they managed it, but they did."

Brightlaw kept his face expressionless. "Why would I know anything, sir?" he asked blandly. "They all hail from Ireland, I understand, and are very probably Catholic. You and I are both Protestants from Boston. You know how that goes. Surely you don't think they'd confide in me."

Umberhine wiped bacon grease from his lips. His stare rested on Brightlaw's face another long moment, as if fiercely trying to probe his thoughts. Given his own brutal treatment of Brightlaw, the man might well be an unspoken ally of the deserters.

At last Umberhine said grudgingly, "Perhaps. Perhaps not. But I do know that incipient grumblings have been spreading through our ranks. God damn it, an officer has to keep a tight rein on these jackals, or they'll defy all authority." He paused, slowly stroking his mustache, still gazing stonily at Brightlaw. Then he said in a surprisingly soft voice, "You know what I have in mind, Seth?"

"I have no way of telling, sir."

Umberhine raised one large hand and stabbed a forefinger at him. "You," he said, "and your two buddies, Pulvermacher and Bitters, will go in pursuit of the deserters. Bring them back."

That threw Brightlaw more than a little off stride. "Sir?"

"You heard me. You three seem to hitch together like train cars. So it'll be even odds. Three of you against three of them. And I can't really spare any more men for such a detail. We'll have all we can do to cope with the situation at San Bernardino."

"And," Brightlaw said tonelessly, "would you like them back dead, sir? Or alive?"

"Don't try to be funny, Trooper."

"I'm not, sir."

"Like hell you're not." Umberhine rose casually to his feet, tucking his thumbs in his belt. "Take 'em any way you can, I don't give a damn. Just run 'em down. I'll take your gentleman's word of honor as to how it goes."

"Yes, sir. And how shall we track them? None of us are any shakes at that sort of thing."

"Easily." Umberhine gestured at the stone-faced Indian, who now rose to his feet.

Wolf Call was into late middle age, his brown face deeply seamed with his years, but his movements were still strong and lithe. His stocky body looked hard and compact under his worn calico shirt, trousers, and knee-length moccasins.

"He's a full-blood Delaware," Umberhine said, "and well qualified to track for you." He smiled wickedly. "You'll be in charge of the patrol, Seth. Don't come back until you find them. I don't care how long it takes."

"Yes, sir," Brightlaw said thickly, fighting back the anger he felt. "But you'll be on the move. How will we find you again?"

"Your guide will see to that. To get back here, all you'll need do is follow the road until you overtake us." Umberhine grinned with an undisguised malice. "You can manage to do that, can't you?"

CHAPTER EIGHT

It was mid-morning before Sergeant Hanrahan stirred awake. He always went to sleep with a cold cigar clamped in his jaws, and by the time he woke it was usually chewed to shreds.

"What's that supposed to be, Sarge?" a flippant trooper had once joshed him. "Your mammy's sugar tit?" but he'd said it only once, and after Hanrahan had beat the daylights out of him nobody ever ventured to say it again.

Hanrahan spat out the soggy remnant of the cigar as he shook off his blankets and heaved to his feet. "Come on, buckoes!" he roared. "Up off your bloody asses! We got plenty of territory to cover today."

Trooper Coyne swore once and rolled up onto his heels, promptly awake and alert, his short, strong body ready for anything. For Trooper O'Flynn, rousing from sleep was a considerable ordeal. He was long and thin and loose-jointed, and he awoke groggily. Watching him get up, bitching steadily and murmurously under his breath, was like seeing a compressed accordion unfold its pleats.

Just watching O'Flynn's laborious rising improved Hanrahan's disposition by a notch or so.

Last night they had managed to slip out of camp without too much difficulty. It was just a matter of situating their gear on a far side of the bivouac and timing the sleepy sentry's rounds of the encampment. Then they had seized up what they needed, including the grub supplies they'd cached nearby, and faded away into the darkness. Their absence

47

probably wouldn't be noticed till dawn, and meantime it was important to put all the distance they could between them and the troop.

O'Flynn blinked surlily. "It's a bit more shut-eye I could stand, Sarge. We'll be facing a long march in the damned sun. Best to lay up by day and travel by night."

"I'm aware of that, scut," Hanrahan said brusquely. "But right now we've got to be thinking of making tracks. Right, Danny?"

"I'd not argue that, Michael." Coyne's square face was expressionless, matching his mild tone. "But d'ye reckon we might be having a bite to eat first?"

"Eat later," Hanrahan said. "Come now, buckoes. We're seasoned to this country. We know where we're goin'. Straight west. And we can feed our faces as we trek."

"Aye," O'Flynn said worriedly. "But how well do we know *this* part o' the country?"

"We don't need to know so much. Keep headin' west, we'll hit the Pacific coast. Not far below, Monterey, I'm reckoning, and I've a compass. Come now, shit-for-brains. We've talked all this over before."

He smiled ingratiatingly to take the bite off the epithet. O'Flynn returned the smile.

Privately, though, Hanrahan shared their worries. They had only a vague idea of how far they were from the ocean. He did have the map he'd painstakingly drawn, going by whatever information he'd been able to assemble, but he had little real notion of what kind of terrain they might have to cross.

They had some cooked beans and bacon and hardtack in their haversacks, and they had a canteen of water apiece. On that an able-bodied man might march for a week, even at a trying pace, if he stretched his rations. Water was another matter. A man's carcass would dehydrate fast in the blazing heat of the Mojave, and they would have to rely on chance to carry them through.

A man might find a spring, if he were damned lucky, or a seemingly dry wash might yield water if he dug deep enough.

(Trouble was, he'd need to be a goddamn Injun to know where to dig.) And under shaded heights, there might be lava troughs or tanks that were catch-basins for rain water.

"It don't appear too promising, even so, Michael," Coyne observed, shrugging his haversack across one shoulder. "But we're with ye. We three struck a vow and we'll keep it. Anything to get away from that Boston-blessed Umberhine. And there'll be no turnin' back now."

"Not unless any of us yearns to be shot." Hanrahan gave O'Flynn a pointed glance. "Aye, the army has no death penalty for desertion in 'peacetime,' so called, but on the other hand, no commander worth his salt ever cavils if a deserter winds up on the wrong end of a bullet. I'm sure we'll not be courting such a fate, Patrick, will we now?"

O'Flynn groaned an assent.

"Let's be moving, then."

All of them were lame and sore from having caught only a few brief hours of sleep on stony soil. Last night they had simply tramped westward by the stars to gain as much distance as possible, until pure exhaustion had forced them to a halt.

Hanrahan had been too dog-tired to assess the nature of the country they were crossing, and it had been pitch-dark except for a nebulous gleam of starlight. Now, as they tramped westward with the sun still at their backs, he began to gain a better and more realistic understanding of what they were up against.

This was a raw and barren terrain, except for a scant lacing of vegetation, largely greasewood. That stuff seemed to flourish everywhere. Hanrahan spotted some *bisnaga*, the barrel cactus whose squeezed-out pulp would provide drinkable liquid if they should need it. Otherwise the sense of desolation was overpowering. He saw rock heights, a scattering of wind-ribbed sand dunes, and a spiraling of black buzzards against the hot blue sky.

The birds gave a man's thoughts an ominous twist. He wondered if they sensed something in advance about the men trekking below them. No . . . hell. Likely they were only cautiously circling down to feast on some carrion prey that was already dead, or close to it.

All the same, the sight of them sent an icy ripple down Hanrahan's backbone.

The men's cramped muscles loosened up as they trudged onward, flexing strength back into their bodies.

But Hanrahan was aware that this was a bare prelude to the terrible ordeal that lay ahead. More and more, he felt shrunk to insignificance by the awful desolation he saw on every side. He felt overburdened by the dead weight of his haversack hung across one shoulder, his heavy Springfield rifle with its makeshift sling across the other.

Maybe he'd been a double-damned fool after all. Maybe he and his companions should have served out their enlistments, as bad as that might have been, rather than attempt to cross the midsummer hell of the Mojave Desert.

It would be a long and harrowing trek, any way you looked at it. Hanrahan had gambled that as they went farther west they were certain to happen on Indian villages and, near the coast, on Spanish missions. Being Catholics, and trained in the rituals to prove it, they should find a warm welcome from the Franciscan fathers. And the isolated Indian bands out here should be peaceable enough . . . outside of the larger factions of Comanche or Kiowa who had already encountered too many sorry dealings at the hands of white men.

All that was reason enough for concern, but Hanrahan's main worry ran deeper. An Irish-hater like Lieutenant Umberhine might well be disposed to send a pursuit patrol after them, and whether the commanding officer of a detail fetched deserters back dead or alive was left to his discretion. Either way, in fact, his troopers would probably be granted several hundred dollars of "subsistence funds." A nice incentive.

Damn and blast, Hanrahan thought bleakly.

For the next several days he and his comrades would have to concentrate mainly on gaining ground and nothing else. Possibly, any pursuit patrol, provided it could pick up the trail, would either lose it somewhere or be slow in picking it up, and then become discouraged after a reasonable length of time.

If we're lucky enough!

They kept on the march until high noon. By then the three deserters were so exhausted they were forced to halt in the shade of some hillside brush. Despite the fact that they were carefully conserving the water in their canteens, the Mojave heat was draining their energies at a fearful rate.

Hanrahan was no coward, but by now he was as close to genuine fear as he'd ever been. A man took his chances when he enlisted in the army: that he'd known in advance. But baking slowly to death under a raw and merciless sun was something he could never have taken into consideration.

At least he had drawn up his makeshift chart of the route. Would it be enough?

After he and his comrades had eaten sparingly of their provisions, Hanrahan squatted on his heels and pulled a map out of his haversack. The stiff paper crackled as he unfolded it. His crude chart of the Mojave Desert was sketched in pencil and included such information as he'd been able to garner by cautious queries he'd dropped here and there, to Army veterans who were older and more seasoned than he was.

He'd drawn XXs to denote mountains, and had placed circles to indicate water holes. Death Valley lay to the north of their proposed route and was only vaguely shown. The Colorado River had been drawn in with extreme care, as had the outline of the Pacific Coast. Some prominent features, such as the Tehachapi Mountains and the San Joaquin Valley, were neatly delineated. But at the location of the many small mountain ranges, such as the Sierra de Salinas, that separated the desert from the ocean, he could make only uncertain guesses.

In any case, Hanrahan explained as he pointed out their prospective route on the map, he was gambling on coming out close to Monterey and then working up the coast to San

Francisco. He'd gone over all this before, but hoped it might lend his tired friends a bit of spirit.

"And then, Michael?" Coyne asked in his mild way.

"We might take passage to the Orient on a clipper ship. Either of you two souls ever had the urge to visit Shanghai?"

Coyne and O'Flynn exchanged glances. Both men said at the same time, "No."

"Likely ye've no good impression of the word," Hanrahan said agreeably. "Granted, the voyage might be a stinkin' ordeal, but it would be a sure way of escaping the clutches of the U. S. Army."

"And then what, Patrick?" murmured Coyne. "What's in store for any of us?"

"Well, we'd return home after a couple years on the high seas, and the Army 'ud no longer be seeking us. And we could go north into Montana or Oregon, wherever. Change our names and build new lives for ourselves." Hanrahan raised a hand, solemnly. "We could do that *now*, o'course. But U. S. Marshals will be out, armed with our descriptions and on the hunt for us. However, after a few years of our being abroad, they'd give up on us. What d'ye say, buckoes?"

"I'm guessing it would have to do for now," O'Flynn said lugubriously. "But how about Canada?"

"That'll not do for me," Coyne said promptly. "British soil won't. The Queen's justice might seek me farther'n you think. The damned Royal Mounties never fail to sniff a man out if they learn his whereabouts. I had to flee Ireland because I was accused of murdering a man, me own stepfather. It'd mean a hangman's noose for me."

Hanrahan beamed at him. "Why, Daniel! I'd never of guessed it, ye've always been so damned closemouthed."

" 'Twas for a good reason," Coyne said gently. "But I'm telling ye, Michael, it was a false accusation."

"Of course, lad, of course." Hanrahan tucked away the map and rose to his feet. He batted dust from his pants, then stretched his massive arms and gave a great jaw-cracking yawn. "Well, we'd best be on our way. . . ."

* * *

The character of the country alternated violently between mountainous and flat. Peaks rose ruggedly and abruptly above broad basins smooth-floored with sand and gravel, and those drained down to central flats. There were more modified areas broken into ridges or lava-like tumbles of rock, but these seemed dwarfed by the spectacular peaks and vast stretches of flats. The lowland vegetation was the ubiquitous greasewood, along with widely spaced creosote and borroweed, with cacti sparingly scattered on rocky slopes.

Hanrahan and his fellows stuck to lower areas, skirting the higher ground wherever they could, and the sergeant kept his compass in hand almost constantly, making frequent references to his inadequate chart. To a degree this enabled them to avoid exhausting climbs, as well as the dense stands of brush that clung to the slopes.

They were a long, long way from their destination, and Hanrahan bitterly wished he had calculated carefully in terms of distance as well as general geography.

By mid-afternoon the sky to the north had taken on a sallow and sickly cast, somewhat like the color of a fading bruise. It wasn't an encouraging sign. Neither was a flat, tan shroud of dust rising along their back trail. It wasn't a dust devil; Hanrahan concluded that this was a party of men.

God *damn*, now! Had the soldier boys got on their trail *this* fast? Of course they had mounts; that would partly account for it.

O'Flynn had nervously taken note of the northern sky, as well as the shroud of dust. "Sarge . . . what d'ye make of them signs?"

Hanrahan came to a halt, shifted the weight of his rifle on his shoulder, and scratched his chin. "I'd be reckoning both mean trouble. That look o' the sky to the north, now, it might be likely a sandstorm is coming on us. I've never seen one, much less been in one. But I've been told it's pure hell when it comes down on ye."

Coyne said, "And that dust on our back trail, Michael? Would it be a pursuit party?"

"That, or hostile Injuns. Either way, buckoes, we'd best size up our best prospects for gettin' out of this alive. . . ."

To the west was a broken upheaval of terrain that, countless ages ago, might have been part of a mountain range. Earthquakes or volcanic explosions, coupled with slow erosion, had whittled it down. It would form a sanctuary of sorts if they could reach it before they were overtaken by a sandstorm or human pursuers. That might be a large "if," but just now it seemed their likeliest chance.

"As ye were, lads!" he barked. "Straight ahead! Keep goin'!"

CHAPTER NINE

THE THREE MEN SLOGGED ONWARD, SINKING ANKLE-DEEP in the residue of the sandstorms that had invaded this country before.

The sallow overcast was deepening and broadening into a murky yellow that swiftly spread across the whole sky, drenching it from one horizon to the other, dimming the sun to a blotch of golden haze and throwing a slow gloom across the landscape. Not a man easily daunted, Hanrahan felt dwarfed by this awesome evidence of nature's might and the potential fury it might unleash.

The flat layer of dust still approached at their backs, overtaking them slowly but surely. By now he could pick out the forms of individual riders, and Hanrahan thought he had his answer. There were too many of them, ten or maybe a dozen, for this to be a force of men that Umberhine could have afforded to put on their trail.

So . . . what about the Mojaves?

Hastily, and somewhat desperately now, Hanrahan scrabbled in his mind to review whatever he could remember about this native tribe.

At present they were raiding heavily in the San Bernardino area. That was unusual in itself. There was little or nothing on record about southwestern Indians concerting for a major attack. It might be the style, on occasion, of northern tribes, but the Indians of this region rarely closed for the kind of mass battle that whites new to this territory had heard stories of in Europe.

Nearly always, these southwestern defenders of their native country would keep up a continual harassment of whites by hit-and-run forays, stealing horses, sniping at their enemies from cover. So it wasn't surprising that once the Indians came across tracks of men wearing boots, they would follow them relentlessly to pick off a handful of the hated white-eyes.

"Lay into it, buckoes!" Hanrahan shouted at his companions. "We want to get into cover directly. . . . Only chance we'll stand."

By now the crumbled tan walls of the ancient formation seemed to loom just ahead, but Hanrahan knew how illusory distances could be on the baking desert.

Round about them, he began to notice, everything had shrunk into a brooding silence. No stir of wind. No movement of any kind. No scuttling of a lizard or flight of a bird. Even the occasonal calls of quail from the deeper brush had died away.

Yet the pall of yellowish heat had worsened, sapping the men's muscles with its terrible force. Hanrahan felt as close to pure panic as he'd ever been.

Now at last, miraculously it seemed, they had almost reached the edge of rocky cover. At the same time the Indians were coming on fast at their backs. He could plainly discern them through the dust, though only as anonymous brown-clad figures.

Whooping savagely, the Indians opened fire. But it was nearly impossible to hit anything from horseback with a rifle, and their intended victims were beyond pistol range.

They had rifles, no doubt ranging from rapid fire Winchesters to old flintlocks. A few might be armed only with bows and arrows, which could be surprisingly effective in the hands of a man seasoned to their use.

That age-old convulsion of earth had caused great rough-blocked boulders to be flung out from the formation, strewn about like children's blocks.

Hanrahan yelled, "Get behind cover fast, boys, and give it to 'em: But hold yer fire till I say the word."

Even as he spoke, he heard a hard-driven grunt from close behind him and looked back. Patrick O'Flynn had caught a bullet in the back. He pitched forward on his face, a bloodstain darkening across the back of his faded blue blouse.

Coyne halted, hesitating as he gazed down at O'Flynn.

"Goddammit, he's done for!" roared Hanrahan. "Hustle your hocks, bucko! *Get to cover!*"

Staggering a few yards farther, both men dropped behind adjacent blocks of tan rock and unslung their .45–.70 Springfield rifles—or "charcoal furnaces," as the regular troopers called them.

These were still standard issue for the U. S. Army. They were powerful and accurate, and superior to the repeating Winchesters. Their main drawback was that a man had to reload after each shot. Also, through spaced repeated firings, the rifle barrel would become too hot to grip.

Hanrahan cocked his weapon and took a careful bead on the Indian in the lead. Would he be the head of this war party? Probably. The warrior was still far away, but if he could pink him just right . . .

Hanrahan fired. The Indian was knocked clean out of his saddle. He rolled over once and didn't move again. It was enough to bring the other Indians to a halt. They were confused, as they always were when they lost a leader.

But they were also angry. The roar of Coyne's rifle spilled another of them to the ground. Then they were piling off their horses, trying to make less obtrusive targets of themselves.

The dust was settling. Hanrahan shot another Indian in mid-stride just after he'd dismounted. Lying on his belly, the warrior continued to lurch himself toward the cover of a small dune.

Quickly reloading, Hanrahan almost shot at him once more but for some reason checked himself. Heathen scut that the savage was, he was also a brave man. Now he was out of the fighting, and Hanrahan would not fire on him again.

By now the Mojaves had taken up positions of sorts behind

shallow rises and were directing a return fire at the two whites.

As Hanrahan peered around the angle of rock and returned fire, bullets caromed in screaming ricochets close to his head. One of them struck the boulder near enough for a rock chip to sting his face, causing him to duck back for a few panicked moments. He swiped a hand across his face where it had struck. It was a slight cut.

Coyne was steadily reloading and shooting. He'd always had a cool head—a man you could depend on. Hanrahan was grateful for that.

Even if the savages knew they were only up against one-shot Springfields, by now they were also aware that their enemies were practiced sharpshooters. So for the present they were cautiously sticking to whatever meager cover they could find.

Hanrahan lost track of time. He and Coyne remained watchful, exchanging occasional shots with the Indians. He could feel the moisture leaking out of his body, drying the tissues, and himself growing perceptibly weaker. It was becoming a sluggish effort of will just to fire his weapon, reload, and fire again. He took a couple of small gulps from his canteen, wanting to stretch the water as far as possible and wondering if, in the end, it would make one damned jot of difference.

All the while he was aware of the approaching sandstorm. In spite of the silent hush around them there was growing thunder from a wave of sand to the north. The weird glow of the sky was fading and darkening under a turgid flood of sand particles that towered hundreds of feet high.

Suddenly the pulsing blanket of heat seemed to loosen, as if it were being pulled up from the ground by invisible wires. An icy wind sent its first hard plummets against them. It chilled to the bone, with a swiftness that was frightening in the wake of the furnace heat.

The first swarm of wind-pelted sand struck. Within moments it would be a fierce blizzard of dry grit that would wipe out all other sights and sounds. Now, thought Hanrahan, would be the time for them to abandon this position and fade back into the larger jumble of broken rock.

"Daniel! Listen now. . . ."

Hanrahan shouted the words, half turning toward his comrade. Even as he did so, Coyne was leaning out a little from his rock shelter to try another shot.

He never got it off. One of the Indians fired in the same instant. The slug took Coyne squarely in the face.

He didn't let out a sound, just slumped forward and sagged to the ground. His face was a bloody mask, but the back of his head was worse. The force of the bullet's emergence had torn out the whole back of Coyne's skull.

Sweet Mary and sweet Jesus.

Hanrahan squatted on his heels, feeling the numb shock of realization sweep through him and then ebb away.

Now he was alone, a lone man against a bunch of blood-hungry hostiles, and his only duty was to get his own hide out alive.

"Ye damned heathen scum!" he screamed, shaking his fist at the enemies in front of him.

It was a futile gesture, and he let it go at that. The wind-lashed flicks of sand bore grittily against his face, but they also lent him a cover of sorts.

Hanrahan climbed to his feet, bent in a half crouch as he wheeled around, tugged his hat tight about his eyes, and raced for the deeper cover of the rocky upheaval.

He was braced for the sound of a shot at any moment, the feel of a bullet slamming into his back. But no shot, no sound, came. The Mojaves must have lost sight of him in the increasing blasts of wind and sand.

Hanrahan stumbled around a massive block and unexpectedly came upon a giant fissure in the facing cliff. It seemed to split the whole escarpment from top to bottom, and he couldn't tell how far back it might extend.

For a moment he hesitated, but then, peering backward through the blowing storm, he saw the dark outlines of men, ducking low against the storm's force as they followed him.

God *damn*! He could find shelter of a sort in this fissure, where they could only come at him one at a time. But he might be backing himself into a dead end as well. The cliffs soared upward almost sheer on either side of him, and they looked unscalable.

A bullet ricocheting off the huge boulder made the decision for him. The savages had him in their sights again; now he must move fast or die on the spot.

The tempest of sand smashed full force against him now, nearly blinding him, obscuring everything. Hanrahan lurched into the fissure, eyes squinted almost shut, one arm flung sideways to feel his way. He fumbled along one rugged wall, not knowing what he might encounter. If the gorge pinched off up ahead, he was trapped for sure.

The deeper he penetrated into the cliff, the less he was punished by wind and sand. That was something. Maybe he could make a stand against the red bastards. They were following him, all right. He could hear an occasional muffled word, pitched below the howling fury of the storm.

There it was. The end of the passage. Blinking through eyelids that felt as though they'd been rasped by sandpaper, he made out the narrowing of the crevasse. If anything lay beyond that, it wouldn't matter. A child might be able to worm farther along, or a lizard or a snake, but a full-grown man couldn't.

Hanrahan flattened his back against the wall, swabbed at his burning eyes with his ragged neckerchief, and fumbled a shell out of his cartridge box. Come on, you red bastards, he thought. I'll make me last stand here.

He saw an Indian stumble into view around an angle in the passage. Hanrahan cocked his rifle, tipped it up, and pulled the trigger. The man folded in mid-stride and fell on his face.

It brought the others momentarily to a halt. Then they pushed forward again as Hanrahan hastily reloaded. His next shot dropped a second warrior across the body of the first.

Whirlwinds of sand were already descending to blow across the corpses, slowing obscuring them from sight. Then another Indian peered around a corner. He fired quickly, too quickly to take good aim, then ducked back. The slug whined off naked rock just above Hanrahan's head.

A fighting grin twisted his lips as he dug out another cartridge, slammed it into the Springfield's breech, and thought, If ye'd rushed me right then, scuts, ye'd of had me! But I'll take a few more of you with me yet. . . .

The Indians didn't advance any farther right away. From their hoarse gibberings in whatever heathen dialect they spoke, he could tell that they were crouching just out of sight beyond the angling rock.

One of them, armed with a repeating rifle, fired off all the rounds in his weapon, a dozen or so shots in as many seconds, blasting at the rock walls.

Hanrahan growled out a fierce chuckle. The heathens were hoping to nail him with a ricochet, but each bullet sang harmlessly off bare rock, never coming near him.

He held his own fire. He'd catch the next man that had the temerity to show himself. . . .

But something else was happening. The intensive crash of gunfire, the boom of echoes, was causing a slow cracking of rock overhead. God *damn*!

A sudden space opened in the cramped wall above as a section of the wall sloughed ponderously away. Christ, it was all coming down on him!

Hanrahan dropped to his hunkers, rifle across his knees, folding his arms over his face, and ducking his head in an attempt to shield himself. Then all sensation died, as a chunk of falling rock smashed against the side of his head.

The din of roaring sand and caving rock was wiped out as he was plunged into unconsciousness.

CHAPTER TEN

THE SANDSTORM OVERTOOK THE PURSUIT PARTY OF Troop B some miles away. None of the three troopers had had any experience of one. But their tracker, Wolf Call, had.

When the first hint of ominous yellow began to sallow the horizon to the north, Wolf Call ordered a halt and told them in broken English what they might expect next, and how to prepare for it.

They rode about a half mile farther till they came to a mass of folded and buckled lava that thrust up above a flat basin floor. Here Wolf Call advised another halt and gave the troopers more terse advice. The horses were to be stripped of their saddle gear, herded into the cover of a deep arroyo, and tethered there. A rude tent of blankets could be propped up on sticks and arranged to form a pocket among the bulges of lava, and the men could stash their gear under its shelter. After they had shoved their saddles and other plunder into the narrow space between lava slabs, they crawled inside under the blankets and sandwiched themselves alongside each other, their backs to the rock.

They were pretty well sheltered from the gathering fury outside—at least so far—and Brightlaw listened closely to Wolf Call's description of how the sandstorm would sweep down.

A quilt of terrific heat had already descended on them, so oppressively that they had to open their mouths to pull enough air into their lungs.

On his right side Brightlaw was flanked first by Idaho Bitters and then by Pulvermacher, and Wolf Call was squeezed in to his left.

At first the Indian's overpowering odor of leather and sweat half suffocated Brightlaw, but he remembered something that an old scout had once told him: "Injuns don't fancy white man's smells any better'n whites do theirs, son."

What the hell. Brightlaw almost chuckled aloud.

He had come from a cultured and curried background, but even a short time in the West had shown him that most white frontiersmen, outside of the regular army, smelled worse than any Indian. At least desert Indians used a kind of soapy cactus pulp to scrub themselves thoroughly. This included their long hair, which they took an inordinate pride in keeping clean and louse-free.

Idaho Bitters dug a silver-colored flask out of his pocket, uncapped it, and took a swig. Then he proffered it to Max Pulvermacher.

"Nein, nein." Pulvermacher pushed it aside with a repelled grimace. "I do not partake of ardent spirits, my friend. You know this."

"Sure I do, Dutchy," Idaho said. "But there's times when you feel your balls mounting clear to your belly. Some tiger sweat might soothe your humors. Don't you feel scared any?"

Pulvermacher boomed a soft laugh. "Sure, I am scared. Who would not be? But that stuff is no answer to it."

"Sure ain't," Idaho said agreeably. "But it do take the edge off a man's nerves. You want a draught of it, Seth?"

"No," Brightlaw said. "Put it away. I'm in charge of this patrol, remember? Hizzoner the lieutenant said so."

"Uh-huh. But I seen you takin' more'n a few sips o' the hard stuff on occasion."

Brightlaw smiled. "On occasion. Not one like this. Mostly what that tarantula juice does is dull your wits. And gives you some nasty feelings when you come out of it. I hope that's all the booze you've packed along."

"Oh, sure. What did you figure? That I'd be dumb enough to fill my canteen with it?"

"No. I didn't figure you'd be *that* stupid."

"Sometime," Wolf Call murmured, "white men have done this. So do Injuns sometime. They all sick with drinking. Bad rotten stuff. It is a sickness."

Wolf Call was stocky and no longer young. Yet somehow, his lined face had a commanding mien and an impenetrable dignity, as though in some way he held himself aloof from these white men and their various machinations. Until now he had hardly deigned to offer the white troopers any comments, outside of those that were necessary to convey needed information.

Feeling a small break in Wolf Call's reserve, Brightlaw said, "You seem to know the desert pretty well. But Lieutenant Umberhine said you're a Delaware. That's a far Eastern tribe. From my country, in fact. I know that some Delawares have come west, but . . ."

Wolf Call's inscrutable face showed the hint of a smile in the daylight that was slowly fading around them, as the sandstorm grew nearer. "Yes. I like Umberhine think that. I like all you white-eyes think that. It is safer for Wolf Call."

"You are saying you're something else?"

"I am Cahuilla," Wolf Call said somberly. "My people, we live here as Mojaves do. We Cahuilla know this land. I trust you white-eyes, I think. I have listen to your talk as you ride with me. You are not much like other soldiers I meet."

So Wolf Call wasn't wholly out of sympathy with them. Brightlaw had suspected that might be so, but he was still curious. "Why does a man like you guide our troops against other Indians?"

"The Mojave, they no friends of ours. Always we fight. But I got nothing to do with fighting now. I lead your pony soldiers to the Mojave, that all."

"You're paid to work for us, I thought."

"I am pay only to scout or guide for you. Not fight."

"Not to fight other Indians, you mean?"

"Mebbeso."

There was a flat finality to the word that made Brightlaw

judge he had gotten all he was likely to get out of Wolf Call. At least for now.

Meantime the approaching sandstorm was increasing in its force and fury. Just as Wolf Call had predicted, the swelling heat had begun to lift sharply. Whip-threads of cold wind were flicking inside their meager shelter of rock and blankets, and they were quickly chilled to the bone.

Waiting for the storm to hit, Brightlaw hunkered forward with his head against his knees and did some hard thinking.

Again he came to the same conclusion he had reached hours ago. Phil Umberhine had sent him and his two closest buddies, Pulvermacher and Bitters, to overtake and recapture the three deserters because he didn't want *any* of them back.

With his usual sense of vindictive irony (which he had in plenty, if not the good sense to accompany it), Umberhine had put the three troopers on the trail because he didn't believe that any of them would come back alive. He hoped the whole damned lot of them, including the deserters, would perish in the pitiless heat of the Mojave.

But why had he sent Wolf Call with them to provide guidance of sorts?

Brightlaw was about to put the question to the Cahuilla when the sandstorm struck in all its thunderous rage.

The men seized hold of the sheltering blankets and clutched them tight. Billows of sand blew in on them. The torrent of wind and sand became a howling pressure that built up against their frail barriers. Their legs and lower bodies were quickly covered by heaping sand, and now they had to use all their energies to keep clear a space around their heads and noses.

Meantime the cold wind grew colder. As hard as a man might try to keep a breathing space around his head, the gritty tempest of sand tore through the thick-weave blankets, grating in his nose and throat even if he could keep his eyes shut tight.

The storm wore on, for a numbing space of minutes that seemed like hours. Finally it died away, so gradually that a man couldn't even be sure when its savagery had been spent.

His brain and nerves had been battered almost beyond feeling.

Wolf Call grunted, "Now we go out," and began to push aside the burden of sand-covered blankets. The three troopers lent what assistance they could, moving with the unsteady motions of drunken men. Their senses had been drowned in a furious maelstrom, their bodies and minds suspended in a nightmarish cocoon between solid earth and a savage sky.

A tinny, ringing sound filled Brightlaw's ears as he clambered out of the hollow. The whole landscape seemed changed. Sand had drifted to cover everything in sight except where, here and there, wind had bared old formations long buried by other storms.

Wolf Call had suggested that each man take a swig from his canteen, explaining that a sandstorm such as the one they'd just endured would suck up every particle of moisture not only from the landscape, but also from a man's body.

The troopers did as he advised, then checked on their horses in the arroyo. The animals were all in good shape, but had to be coaxed in patient stages out of the arroyo. They were skittish and spooked. Sand had piled up almost to their knees—their riders had at least been well sheltered from the storm. Brightlaw ordered the men to swab their mounts' nostrils clean of grit.

"Now we go on," Wolf Call said as they loaded the gear back on their animals. "Think maybe we catch up pretty soon."

"But all their track is blown over," Brightlaw said. "How can you be sure?"

"No sure. But track go same way so long as we follow. Straight west. There is sun, too. That help me follow."

Brightlaw nodded. The sun was out again now that the tan haze had dissipated, and he had his compass to help him check on Wolf Call's word. So far the Cahuilla hadn't steered them wrong.

"All right," Brightlaw said. "Let's get going." He glanced at Idaho Bitters, who was looking pretty grumpy as he cinched the latigo around his horse's belly. "I'd guess you have no more of that painter sweat left, have you, chum?"

"Nary a damn drop," Idaho said surlily. "Sucked 'er all down during the storm."

"Still, my friend," Max Pulvermacher said slyly, "we are all still alive. That is something, eh?"

"Hell, you got twice my brains and then some, Dutchy. Whada *you* think?"

"Damn lucky, I think we are," Pulvermacher said, his voice touched with soberness now. "It is always something, when a man stays alive, no matter what else happens to him. . . ."

Each man took a drink of the carefully conserved water in his canteen. Then they took up the trek westward, across a now barren vista.

Phil Umberhine might have been correct, Brightlaw thought grimly. This patrol could well prove to be tantamount to a death sentence. It would be a tricky business even to pick up their own back trail from the point where the storm had caught them.

How well had Hanrahan and the other deserters come through it? Maybe they hadn't.

Brightlaw fully intended to find them and take them alive, if possible. He was a voluntary enlistee in the United States Army and—by his own code of ethics—was bound to its rules. Umberhine had said he'd "take your gentleman's word of honor as to how it goes," but Brightlaw wondered just how much that avowal really meant. After all, what reason did he have to trust Phil?

Pulvermacher rode close beside Wolf Call as they moved west. Unbending a bit under Max's ceaseless barrage of questions, the Cahuilla pointed out and named the plants that grew in scattered patches. Smoke trees, *palo verdes*, even some isolated stands of palm trees.

"One thing I see," Pulvermacher observed. "These trees do not grow close to the greasewood."

"Greasewood is poison," Wolf Call said. "Poison any other plant grow close to it."

"*Ach!* So that would explain it." Pulvermacher tipped his hat to the back of his pale, short-cropped hair and swabbed his sweaty face with his bandanna. "I never liked cold weather, but some winter I would not mind now."

"Winter worse on Mojave," Wolf Call said soberly but with the trace of a smile. "Not so much snow, but cold. Much cold. Wind blow all time."

"*Mein Gott!* What a country."

"Not all bad. The smoke trees you see?"

"*Ja.* They look like smoke from a fire. From a distance, I think."

"Sure. You spot them like that. They grow along dry streambed. You see smoke trees, mebbeso you dig in ground, find water."

"This I like to know." Pulvermacher was always eager to add to his store of knowledge. "And that tree over there"— he pointed—"I have never seen anything like it."

For that matter it was the oddest-looking plant Brightlaw had ever seen, too. About three times the height of a man, yet crabbed and twisted, it bore what seemed to be clusters of sharply pointed blades rather than leaves.

"What you white men call Joshua tree," Wolf Call said. "Very old. Mebbeso oldest thing on earth."

Pulvermacher's face brightened. "*Ach!* This I have read of, even in the Old Country. It is called *Yucca brevifolia.*"

Wolf Call shook his head, baffled. "You get that from white man book?"

"*Ja!*"

Wolf Call shook his head again. Brightlaw reined alongside them, grinning. "My friend studies many things," he told the Cahuilla. "Sometimes I study, too."

"Hunh. What you study?"

"Men, mostly." Brightlaw jogged along in silence for a moment, then added mildly, "I have been studying on why Lieutenant Umberhine sent you with us on this patrol. He doesn't like us."

"I see this. No like me, neither."

"May I ask why not?"

Wolf Call shrugged. "Mebbeso, like you white-eyes say, I get too smart for my britches. I tell Umberhine I am Delaware. Then he tell me his grandfather's father was kill by a Delaware. This happen long time ago. But he no forget."

No. Phil wouldn't forget, not when he knew that Delaware Indians had scattered throughout the West, far from their native haunts, intermingling with other tribes. He'd be the kind to ride a grudge, however senseless, until Hell froze over. This new knowledge confirmed Brightlaw's earlier suspicion: Umberhine had taken an unreasoning hatred to Wolf Call and would as soon see him dead as he would Seth or any friend of his.

They spotted more of the weirdly twisted Joshua trees on the landscape, and Wolf Call said this meant they were climbing to higher ground. Most of the wind-drifted sand was lower down, filling swales and pockets.

At Wolf Call's advice they dismounted and led the horses, plodding doggedly through deep sand. They must spare the animals any needless exertion. By now, the Cahuilla said again, they would be getting close to the deserters. But with the timeless patience of a desert-bred Indian he reckoned that *when* they caught up with Hanrahan and his fellows made little difference. The important thing in the here-and-now was not to let their horses founder.

It seemed like sensible advice to Brightlaw, yet he felt his spine starting to tingle with tension. He couldn't remember feeling such a sensation before. It was as though some menace—nothing that a man could really put a finger on—lurked somewhere nearby.

He noticed that Wolf Call, too, seemed to sense something afoot. The Cahuilla said nothing, but his head was up, his nostrils faintly flaring.

Idaho Bitters was grumbling, "Well, gents, this is one helluva vicious lot to go through for eighteen dollars a—" He stopped in mid-sentence and whirled around, his eyes glaring wildly, both hands lifted to clutch at his throat.

A silently fired arrow had caught him in the neck, the shaft projecting from either side. He made a horrible gurgling sound through his open mouth. Then his hands fell away and he pitched slowly forward on his face.

"Over there!" Brightlaw yelled, pointing at a nearby outcrop. Both he and Pulvermacher grabbed hold of Idaho on either side, scooping him to his feet.

Wolf Call brought his rifle to his shoulder and began firing steadily at a sudden blaze of gunfire from a nearby ridge, as the rifle of an unseen enemy now joined the flight of arrows.

They must be damned close. Arrows were hardly effective beyond a range of sixty yards. Fortunately, Wolf Call was armed with a repeating Winchester, not the standard single-shot army Springfield. He fired at the enemy as Brightlaw and Pulvermacher dragged their hit comrade to shelter.

They flopped down behind the shallow outcrop, and a moment later Wolf Call bounded into place beside them. Temporarily, at least, they were out of the line of enemy fire.

With Idaho's back propped against the outcrop, Pulvermacher tore open his collar, staring at the wound. Blood was gushing from it in rhythmic torrents. Brightlaw knew that the German had studied medicine in both Heidelberg and Vienna—the leading medical capitals of the world—so he held himself silent for the moment it took Pulvermacher to settle back on his heels, his face gray and glistening.

"God damn it, Max!" Brightlaw yelled. "How bad? *How bad is it?*"

"As bad as can be," Pulvermacher said between his teeth. "His carotid artery has been cut in two. Idaho, he is finished, Seth."

CHAPTER ELEVEN

HANRAHAN STIRRED, OR TRIED TO. BLOTCHES OF UNCON-
sciousness sifted back into his brain before he came sluggishly awake.

He was sealed in a blanket of sand and fallen rock. That's
why he could hardly move. He was in a sitting position but
buried up to his neck, his mouth and nose barely topping the
sand. A terrible throb of pain filled the side of his head where
the piece of rock had struck him.

He sent a cautious glance down the fissure to where he
had seen the two Indians he had shot fall down. Either their
bodies had been taken away or they were covered by a mound
of wind-blown sand. Most likely, given the customs of these
desert heathens, they had borne their dead away. Now all
was silent and unmoving, and Hanrahan could only guess
that for some reason the Indians had retreated, leaving the
unconscious white man unmolested.

Maybe they'd thought he was dead, or close to it, or maybe
the sandstorm's fury had driven them off. Well, what the hell.
He was alive.

Gingerly, Hanrahan flexed his fingers and toes, then his
arms and legs. Some chunks of rock had plunged down from
the fissure's rim after he'd lost consciousness, but he seemed
to have been partly cushioned by the sand and none of his
bones had been broken. He might have a few bruises, but
other than that godawful agony in his head he felt no pain at
all.

Slowly and carefully, Hanrahan eased himself free of the

choking mass of rubble. He freed his arms first and then pawed laboriously at the heaped rock and sand that pinned his lower body. Finally he could move his legs, and then he was able to stand and fully extricate himself, pulling one leg free and then the other.

Damn. Where was his rifle? He couldn't afford to lose that.

He was lucky. A little scrabbling in the mounded sand uncovered his Springfield. It would have to be carefully cleaned before it would be serviceable again. Hanrahan swore feelingly.

He wanted nothing more than to be on his way west. It was a sorry thing about Coyne and O'Flynn, but all three men had deserted with a full awareness of the hazards they might encounter.

Go forward, then. Never look back. He relieved his burning thirst with a last swig of water from his canteen.

Dizzy from his head wound, Hanrahan cast a dim glance over his shoulder as he lurched away from the pile of rock and sand.

What he saw stopped him in his tracks.

Just inside the lee of the cave lay the remains of a human body. It was the skeleton of a man, clad in a metal suit of some kind. Hanrahan had to blink his eyes several times before he could believe what he saw.

The bones were all that remained of an incredibly large man, and his outfit looked like the armor of an ancient Spanish conquistador. The breastplate that girdled his upper trunk was made of ancient iron or steel, and the helmet that lay beside him was of hammered brass, no less. All of it was dented and pitted and covered with a deep skin of rust.

Christ and all the saints, Hanrahan thought with a crushing sense of awe. He even crossed himself, something he hadn't bothered to do in a dozen or more years.

Long ago—perhaps several centuries—this man had sought shelter in the cave, only to be trapped by a fall of rock from above. Possibly it had come down as the result of an earthquake or other natural force. Whatever, it had trapped him here, and here he had died. It had taken the sudden shock of gunfire to break free the rock and liberate the corpse.

Hanrahan stood paralyzed for about a quarter minute, and then he was scrambling across the pile of rubble to reach the ironclad bones. The man had died in a contorted position, twisted on his side. Underneath the bones of one outflung hand was a large leather pouch, which he must have gripped until the last, until he'd passed out from lack of air. At his other side lay the corroded husk of what appeared to be an ancient matchlock musket.

The leather bag had become stiff and rotted with the passing of time. When Hanrahan reached out to extract it from beneath the skeletal hand, it fell to pieces. But what spilled out of the cracked leather set Hanrahan's pulse thumping, and the misery in his head throbbing even worse.

Jesus! It was gold!

Big nuggets of solid gold, larger than he had ever seen— perhaps forty or so. Altogether, they represented more wealth than Michael Hanrahan, descendant of Irish bog-trotters that he was, could ever have hoped to see at one time.

He picked up the chunks of gold in his thick hands, fondling them one at a time before he laid them carefully down, his mind stunned. *My God!* Here was the answer to all his needs . . . the need for money, for an escape to a new life.

All he had to worry about now was how he could get himself, along with the gold, out of this damned desert.

Hell, I can do it! There was no room for doubt in Hanrahan's mind. Still he hesitated, gazing down at the ancient Spaniard's bones and rusted armor. How in God's name had the fellow come to be here?

Hanrahan was no scholar, but he had a fairly sharp memory. Digging down into long-buried memories from his schoolboy days, he remembered being taught about Francisco Vásquez de Coronado. Even if he was a Spaniard, the man must have been Catholic, and a bold explorer to boot. Coronado had sent a mixed army of Spanish cavalry and Indian allies into what was now New Mexico, where reports of a new wealth-rich country to the north had brought him onto the Great Plains. Bewildered by the vastness of the country, Coronado had ordered his main force of men back to Mexico, while he himself had led some fifty horsemen as far north as the great bend of the Arkansas River in Kansas. There he had given up the quest and returned to Mexico.

This spot, Hanrahan knew, was far to the west of Coronado's route. If this fellow had been of his command, how had he come to be here? And why had he taken refuge in this precarious niche?

Hanrahan had his share of Celtic imagination, and he could easily conjure up any number of answers. If the Spaniard had somehow come on such a quantity of gold by himself, and had wanted to keep it all, his life would have been in danger from his equally avaricious comrades. If they had learned of such a mess of gold, as they were bound to, his solution might have been boldly to desert the command and strike out on his own, trusting on blind luck to carry him through.

His great size and a powerful constitution had gotten him this far. Then, much the same could have happened to him as had happened to Hanrahan. A sandstorm, or hostile Indians, might have driven him to this refuge. Maybe he'd been wounded. An earth tremor, a wee earthquake, or perhaps even the firing of his own matchlock had brought down the overhanging rock, trapping him.

Ah . . . all very pretty to speculate on, but he'd never have the real answer, Hanrahan knew. Right now he meant to examine his own precarious situation a bit more completely.

He clambered out of the fissure, pausing only to dig deep enough into the mounded sand to verify that the dead Indians had been carried away by their fellows. But why had the heathen left him alive? Abruptly Hanrahan understood why. The sudden exposure of the armor-clad skeleton must have rattled their superstitious sensibilities.

Slogging onward through the sand, Hanrahan sought and found the nearly buried body of Coyne. And a little farther on, that of O'Flynn. He dug out their canteens and poured what little water was left into his own canteen. He also appropriated their remaining provisions and their cartridge boxes. Afterward, all he could do was heap a bit more sand to wholly cover their bodies and bow his head.

Ah God, poor lads . . . and it was Michael Hanrahan who'd led them to this fate. Perhaps something should be said above their remains: The orderly way would be a commital prayer, an office of the dead performed, but Hanrahan was (God knew!) no priest, and somehow, under these conditions, the whole business would have seemed grotesque.

Let the dead rest as they were.

There was still the gold. And by the saints, he would pack it out of here, every damned ounce of it, and begin his new life. Even if he were to die in the attempt.

Just the thought sent a burning rush of energy through Hanrahan's veins. He tramped back to the fissure and swung into it. Even as he did so, he heard an ominous rumble of sound from one side. A deep, grinding noise of rotted rock separating itself from other rotted rock.

He froze in place, waiting till the gentle rumbling subsided.

He licked his cracked lips. Up ahead, where the falling rock had exposed the ancient skeleton, more rock was on the verge of coming down. Anyone caught underneath it would be buried alive . . . and centuries from now someone might find his own bones next to those of the old conquistador.

Hanrahan wiped a furrow of sweat from his brow. Couldn't afford to sweat. He'd need all his body water for the unknown miles ahead. But by God, he was going after that gold. It's mine by right of discovery, he thought, and I'll have it all!

Obscurely he knew that his mind was no longer functioning rationally; maybe his brain was getting fevered. It didn't matter. He was going ahead.

Hanrahan shed the weight of his haversack, settling it gently on the ground. Then, very slowly and carefully, he picked his way forward into the fissure across the heaped sand and rubble.

Another loud crack sounded from the overhanging rock, causing him to come to a dead halt. By now he was again in sight of the small cave where the long-dead Spaniard reposed. Scattered in the rubble beside it were the gold nuggets that had burst out of the rotted leather bag.

Hanrahan lowered himself slowly to his hands and knees and painstakingly crawled the remaining distance, careful not to let his booted feet knock against any protruding fragment of rock. Even a slight reverberation of sound might bring down the whole wall.

Best not to think on it anymore. Just go ahead.

Hanrahan inched up to the cave opening and then, settling on his haunches, began to gather up the nuggets, stuffing them inside his shirt.

God, but the stuff was heavy! Pure gold must be the heaviest metal in the world. How had that soldier of old managed to pack it this far through the desert heat?

Another groaning of rock from above. Ah, Christ! He was right underneath it now, and maybe he'd do best to clear out while he still could. But pure greed impelled Hanrahan to continue gathering up the nuggets and jamming them into his shirt.

More noises of splitting rock overhead. A fine sifting of earth fell on his head and back. His whole body jerked with the soft warning impact.

All right. He had collected all but few of the nuggets, and he'd best be getting out. It took all of Hanrahan's self-control for him to force himself to crawl slowly from the spot, again on his hands and knees. But the rumble of separating rock overhead had suddenly increased, and the earth was quaking beneath him.

Hanrahan lunged to his feet and lumbered forward. The weight of gold in his shirt caused him to stumble and fall. With an immense effort he heaved back to his feet and lurched on, just as a broad stretch of wall behind him came crashing down.

It descended in several huge chunks, and he was nearly deafened by its roar. He stumbled again, falling on his face. He covered the back of his head with his folded hands and breathed a silent prayer. A few fragments of rock bounced on his body. Then he heard nothing but silence.

Choking on dirt, he lifted his head and peered backward. The avalanche was over. As the dust settled, he saw that the cave was buried from sight once more. Slabs of rock covered it, and likely the old Spaniard had been laid to his last rest.

Coughing, Hanrahan staggered laboriously to his feet and tramped toward the mouth of the fissure. Coming to his haversack, he knelt and opened his shirt, dumping all the nuggets out on the ground. Squatting on his heels, he took the time needed to wipe his Springfield, carefully cleaning all the grit out of its mechanism as well as he could.

His head was still spinning dizzily as he bundled up the gold in his soogan blanket and slung it over one burly shoulder, his canteen and haversack over the other.

His sorry excuse for a chart might still be of use to him, and he still had his compass.

Hanrahan got to his feet. A kind of silent triumph swelled in his throat. He had it now. Nearly all the damned gold, and—if he could muster the strength to manage it—the determination to find his way out of this damned desert . . .

CHAPTER TWELVE

BRIGHTLAW AND HIS COMPANIONS HADN'T ACHIEVED A very secure cover. The rough outcrop was a couple of yards wide and maybe two feet high. Now, with no need to attack in silence, the Indians—Mojaves, or whatever they were—opened up with a concerted rifle fire. Bullets sang in screaming ricochets off the top of the outcrop.

Brightlaw and Pulvermacher pulled Idaho Bitters's body down flat on the ground and hunkered beside it, their rifles at the ready.

Brightlaw said to Wolf Call, "Where are they? I think over by that sharp rise, but did you see their powder smoke? I don't want to stick my head out. . . ."

"They fifty yards mebbeso ahead of us." Wolf Call paused as he rapidly reloaded his Winchester. "Not sure just how you white-eyes figure. But they can move around, mebbeso get behind us. We stuck here. No move nowhere else or they get us sure."

He was right. The outcrop was pretty well isolated from any other cover. If they stirred from behind it, they would be easy targets. Brightlaw ducked his head beneath a flurry of splinters from the rotted stone as bullets exploded against it.

"How many of them do you think there are?"

"Enough kill us if they circle," Wolf Call said. "Three, four of 'em, mebbeso, got rifles. I tell from the shots, unh?"

"Well we can't stay nailed down here, then." Brightlaw's voice sounded unreasonably calm in his own ears.

"Mebbeso we no got to."

"How do you mean?"

Wolf Call had laid his head against the outcrop, as though he were listening intently. Afterward he stuck his head out momentarily from the shelter, then pulled it back again just as a crash of gunfire dislodged chunks of rotted rock from where he had briefly exposed himself.

"They get ready come on us from straight front." Again Wolf Call laid one ear against the outcrop. "I hear 'em. They move around some, but I think they get ready make charge on us."

"*Ach,*" Pulvermacher murmured ironically. "Crazy they must be, then. We shoot them all before they get to us, *ja?*"

"You white-eyes have something," Wolf Call said with perhaps a flick of contempt, "when you do dumb things. You call it honor. Is no different. Plains Injuns, they count coup. Desert Injuns, they no do that. But all men do dumb things for 'honor.' "

The Cahuilla's tone suggested that he considered "honor" in all warfare a lot of damn fool nonsense, whether white men committed it or Indians did. Maybe he was right, Brightlaw thought as he crouched tensely on his hunkers, his rifle cocked and ready. What honor was there when men were killed? Whether they had followed some unspoken code of ethics or no rules at all, either way they were just as dead.

Brightlaw felt sweat gliding down his ribs, along his legs, puddling in his boots. He looked up at the sun, now a fuzzy ball of fire in the clear midday sky, so intense that you wouldn't have guessed a sandstorm had blotted it out a short time before.

Brightlaw's eyes ached from the glare; he turned them downward. Without raising his head he followed Wolf Call's example and put his ear against the rock. Could he pick it out, too?

By God, he could. A sudden light thud of moccasined feet quaking through the ground. He glanced swiftly at Wolf Call, who nodded once then rose cautiously to his feet. He crouched low, just enough for his head to clear the rock, rifle at his shoulder.

Brightlaw and Pulvermacher rose too. All three of them fired at the same time.

A half dozen brown-clad figures, Mojave from the look of them, had piled out from behind an abutment of rock no more than fifty yards away. They were racing forward toward the outcrop.

Three of them went down, their bodies flung over backward, floundering in the loose sand before they were still. Wolf Call kept up a steady methodical fire while his two white comrades frantically slammed fresh loads into the breeches of their single-shot Springfields.

The remaining three Indians wheeled and fled at a run for cover, but Wolf Call brought down another of them. Then Brightlaw fired, bringing his man down on the spot.

One wounded Mojave got back to the partial cover, flinging himself down behind it. This was a low, flat outcrop that barely concealed him from their fire. But it was enough.

Wolf Call leaned his head against the outcrop again. After a moment he announced, "Now they all gone but that one we just see. If there was more, they come at us, too."

He looked at the last man he had hit, took a careful aim, and shot him through the head. The Indian jerked, gave a long shuddering moan, and then was silent.

Brightlaw, a little shocked, said, "Why did you do that?"

"He not dead," the Cahuilla said phlegmatically. "He not hit at all. He get really hit, he go down like he knocked over. Same like if he get kicked by white man mule."

Brightlaw rose slowly and shakily to his feet, swiping the back of his hand across his sweat-stinging eyes. Then he looked sharply at Wolf Call. "I thought you wouldn't fight other Indians . . . but you've killed three."

"Unh. When I say that?"

"Well, I guess you didn't, really. But—"

"Any man try kill me, I try kill him first. That is all."

Brightlaw let out a long sigh and settled wearily down on his heels again.

As he did so, he saw a flicker of movement beyond the outcrop where the wounded Mojave had taken shelter. Then he saw the man haul himself to his feet with a dogged effort, using his rifle as a brace for his weight.

Wolf Call raised his rifle to draw a bead, but Brightlaw reached out a hand and batted the piece down. "No!" he said fiercely. "No!"

The Cahuilla glanced at him without malice, somewhat wonderingly. "No kill this one?"

"No, goddammit! Look at him."

The Mojave was fully on his feet now, and he turned and looked their way with fearless defiance, though his face was set against a ferocious onset of pain. With his rifle stock still braced against the ground, standing in plain view now, he raised his other hand clenched in a fist and held it out in a gesture of pure defiance.

Wolf Call fingered his rifle thoughtfully, and Brightlaw said flatly, "Don't."

"Why not? He kill your friend, hunh? Him or another. Enemy is enemy."

"This one's nothing of the sort now. . . . Look at him."

The Mojave wheeled away now, turning with a vast painful effort and using his rifle as a kind of awkward crutch. He began to head away from them, limping badly. A stained red kerchief was tied around his forehead, marking him apart from his companions. His right leg must have been shattered, for it dragged uselessly behind him.

"Still enemy," Wolf Call said implacably.

"And you still want to kill him."

"Yes. But no do if you say no. You lead this patrol."

"That's not really the point. He's helpless—no danger to us now. You don't just wipe a man out for . . ." Brightlaw paused, shaking his head again. He was talking to a different culture—a different set of values.

"You white-eyes kill," Wolf Call observed tonelessly. "You kill a million men, I hear, in a war that last this many years." He held up four fingers. "When you ever hear Indians do that?"

"But that was different! It was . . ."

Brightlaw broke off, seeing the glint of amusement in the Cahuilla's eyes.

"He is right," Pulvermacher declared phlegmatically. "It is all the same. They kill us and they kill people of their own race. Like we do."

"It's not the same, Max!"

"Ach," sighed Pulvermacher. "It never is. But they are all dead. All the brave young men."

The Mojave was still limping away, his head bent, the bad leg dragging behind him, agonizing over each step. From the blood that dyed his legging, the leg bone appeared to have been broken close to the hip. Obviously he expected to catch a bullet in the back at any moment. But the expected didn't come, and he at last made it to the top of a rise. Not looking back, he passed over it and then was lost to sight.

Wolf Calf looked at Brightlaw and said calmly, "I think you be sorry for this."

"Bullshit!" Brightlaw exploded. "Why should I be? He's on his last legs. How far will he get?"

"Mebbeso got horse nearby. If he reach it . . ."

"He'll never be able to get on it. So what the hell difference does it make?"

"How you know? Mebbeso his medicine is strong. Mebbeso you see him again, with others. Then you be sorry, Brightlaw."

CHAPTER THIRTEEN

AFTER DIGGING A SHALLOW GRAVE IN THE LOOSE SAND and laying Idaho Bitters to his last rest, the three men left the cover of the outcrop and ventured cautiously out to the open terrain. They didn't bother to bury the Mojaves they had shot down, but did appropriate the Winchester rifles that two of them had carried, along with their ammunition.

That's how it often was with the Army of the West. Frequently the hostiles were armed with fifteen-shot repeating Winchesters, or maybe Henrys, while the regular army was still issuing standard single-shot Springfields to its troops. The Springfields had no equal when it came to accuracy and hard-hitting firepower, but the troopers were always at a disadvantage when they had to face enemies who were armed with rapidfire repeaters.

Brightlaw straightened up and stretched his arms, feeling his cramped muscles crack with the effort, as he gazed around him. In a brief space of time the storm of wind-lashed sand had changed the whole landscape, obscuring all its details. Bigger landmarks still stood out plainly. And the back trail of tracks left by the Mojaves who had laid up an ambush for them was still clear.

He looked at Wolf Call. "Seems they came here from the west."

The Cahuilla nodded. "Mebbeso we follow track so far as where sandstorm cover track. I think it same way your deserters go."

The three men spent some time trying to round up their

horses, who had been spooked away by the gunfire, but the animals had strayed too far. They were lost somewhere in the vast wasteland. Perhaps they could be tracked down, but Brightlaw didn't think the three of them could spare the time to attempt it.

"We have our orders," Brightlaw said curtly, "and we have our duty. We still have three deserters to run down."

Pulvermacher shrugged resignedly. "*Ach.* So how we go is what you say. You the head of this patrol are."

Brightlaw smiled crookedly. "Sure. That's what hizzoner Lieutenant Umberhine told me. So we'll go ahead. Try to fulfill our goddamned duty . . . ."

It seemed that the party of Mojave had also lost their horses in the sandstorm.

Wolf Call had no difficulty following the Mojaves's foot trail west, until again all sign petered out at the point where the sandstorm had obliterated their tracks. But just a short distance beyond they came to a fissure in a looming wall of rock.

Even Wolf Call couldn't be sure of what had happened at this point. The blowing sand had drifted over practically all the sign. The Cahuilla went over the ground thoroughly and concluded that the three deserters might have been driven to this place by a combination of the sandstorm and some pursuing Indians.

They couldn't tell anything for sure. But the party of Mojaves that Brightlaw and his companions had come up against might have been survivors of an earlier encounter with the deserters.

The trampled track showed that one man, at least, had made his way out of the fissure, and then had struck out due west.

One man? Brightlaw did some puzzling over that. The Indians would have carried off their own dead, if any. But two of the deserters must have been wiped out, their bodies immured by the drifting sand. Yet . . . which one of them had survived?

As long as even one remained at large, it was Brightlaw's duty to track him down. The funnel-shaped prints the man had left in the deep, loose sand would be easy to follow.

Wolf Call agreed that they should do this, observing that their big problem would be to find enough water to carry them through the mission. He could find water, he was confident, for prominent landmarks that he'd known all his life still reared above the altered swales and other low spots. But if they were constrained to follow the track left by the lone survivor, they wouldn't dare go far off it to find water.

"Then we'd better get going," Brightlaw said, fighting the drag of weariness and the sapping heat. "How much chance of finding water in this direction?"

"Not sure," replied the Cahuilla. "There desert tanks, big basins in solid rock collect water. But mebbeso these all fill with sand. I see this happen sometime."

It was an accurate surmise. Chihuahua Tanks, about a mile farther, was filled to the rim with sand, as though the dry sandstorm had sucked up every drop of moisture even before the full fury of blowing sand had struck.

It was a miserable trek, in any case. Even the relatively slight weight of their weapons and other gear tugged at their muscles. Despite the dryness of the atmosphere (no humidity to worry about), all three men were sweating plentifully, even if Wolf Call stood up better under the awful heat than his white companions.

"Not try go fast," he cautioned them. "Put pebble in mouth. Work up spit, not get so thirsty then."

Good advice. But it worked only so far. Several times they had to call rest halts and slack down in the meager shade of whatever abutments of rock were to be found, gathering their strength for another tedious stretch of marching. The toughest area was a dry soda lake where the sandstorm appeared to have reached its westernmost swath, leaving only a clean-swept surface in which the fugitive's tracks were barely visible.

After crossing it, they came onto higher ground dotted

with the crabbed Joshua trees and isolated stands of creosote
brush. There were also dozens of black cinder cones, some
of them several hundred feet high, each with a central crater.
The tremendous pressure of erupting lava—probably thou-
sands of years ago—had blown open most of the craters on
one side.

The sun had heeled over well to the west when Brightlaw
tiredly lifted one hand to signal a final halt.

They would lie up here and get some sleep through the
night hours. Even Wolf Call's desert lore wouldn't help them
to follow any more track today.

Wolf Call rounded up enough brush and wood to build a
campfire, while Brightlaw and Pulvermacher made bivouac
on the spot and warmed up what few food supplies they had
to provide a supper of sorts.

The two whites sat back in the lengthening shadows and
dropped their chins against their drawn-up knees. They exchanged a few desultory remarks and watched the orange orb
of the sun descend to the horizon, throwing a reddish glow
across the landscape.

Brightlaw groped through the tangle of his thoughts and
found a fine ribbon of anger threading them. Not against
Wolf Call or Pulvermacher, but against himself.

Tiredly, he raised his chin off his knees. "Max?"

"*Ja?*"

"We've known each other awhile. But we've never ques-
tioned each other . . . about our pasts. You know something
of mine, now."

"*Ja.* Of Umberhine and his wife and how it was with you.
Not all of it, maybe, but enough."

"Yes. I'm a closemouthed guy, usually. So are you."
Brightlaw felt an embarrassed warmth in his face, but he'd
started the train of speculation and it was too late not to
follow through. "What I wanted to say is . . . you're not
sympathetic toward wars or why men wage them. You left
the old country to escape being drafted."

Pulvermacher's burly shoulders heaved in a quiet chuckle.
"*Ja.* And you want to know how I wound up in the army."

"Well, I . . . Hell, it's none of my business."

"Fair is fair, Seth. Tit for tat. I would not tell anyone else, but you I will." Max paused, rasping a hand over his burr of blond whiskers. "Over here, in America, I for a time live in New York City. Here were people from many lands, but I, an ignorant German by the American standards, what do I know? I am built like a workhorse, but all I care about is things of the mind. I come from a good family; my father insists that I attend medical schools. This was good with me. There the saving of life is taught, not the taking of it. But this means nothing in a new country. Bavaria I had fled as a fugitive from the Kaiser's law. I have no credentials for practice here. I have no money, either. My family would not send me any. They consider me a disgrace to the *Vaterland*. So finally . . . my back is against the wall, only one thing is left to me."

Brightlaw didn't have to guess. "The army. They'll take on anyone and ship him out to duty, if he's able-bodied."

"*Ja*. This is not how you came by it, but in some ways we both were forced, eh?"

Brightlaw jerked a laugh out of his chest. "Yeah. You've said it, Max. . . ."

Wolf Call returned suddenly, but empty-handed. And he was moving fast. As usual his face was stoical, as if graven in stone. All the same, Brightlaw sensed a trace of grim excitement in his demeanor.

Brightlaw got to his feet, grimacing against the old pain in his lower back and rubbing it with both hands. "What is it?"

"I find him," Wolf Call said.

"What? Who?"

"Man we follow. Sergeant Han-ran."

"Hanrahan?"

"There." Wolf Call pointed with his chin, as every Indian that Brightlaw had ever met always did. "Over hill there. He pass out. No get no farther."

Brightlaw and Pulvermacher scrambled after the Cahuilla as he led them up a short slope and through the scrub brush.

On the other side of the shallow rise they found the body of First Sergeant Michael Hanrahan, sprawled on its side.

He was unconscious, not dead. But the strain of getting this far showed on his sunburned and whiskered face. It was turned sideways out of the dirt, his mouth hanging open, the swollen tongue dangling out of one corner.

They had caught their man. But even that fact didn't seize their dulled attention right away. Hanrahan had been toting a bundled blanket over his shoulder, and most of it had spilled out when he'd collapsed.

Gold. Maybe a small fortune of it, pure nuggets of it, lay scattered on the ground. Red-gold glints of fading sun glanced off the rough surfaces.

Pulvermacher raised his awed stare to meet Brightlaw's. *"Mein Gott,"* he whispered.

CHAPTER FOURTEEN

As soon as the men got over their first excitement, they carried Hanrahan down to the proposed campsite. Then they went back and gathered up his gear and, of course, the gold. Brightlaw packed the nuggets back into the blanket and carried it down, too.

God, it made a weight across a man's shoulder! He wondered how and where Hanrahan had come across it, and how far he had borne it. Even for a man of his bull-like stamina it would be a hell of a load to tote very far. Hanrahan might have picked it up somewhere near the deep fissure where his boot tracks had been renewed after the sandstorm had ceased.

But how he had found it was a mystery, and might remain so. In any event he might have tramped farther than he had if not for the weighty burden.

They still had to scour up a supply of firewood before the last sunlight completely faded. Wolf Call went out again on the wood-fetching detail. While he was gone, Max Pulvermacher gave Hanrahan a thorough examination.

"He is in bad shape, but I do not think is wounded, Seth," Pulvermacher said. "No bones are broken. But there is this." He traced a finger around the great crusted patch of blood on one side of Hanrahan's scalp. "There he was hurt."

"Not a bullet wound, then?"

"*Ach.* I think not. It is like something hit him, but no bullet. I think some time ago it happen. *Himmel!* How could a man come so far, bearing all that gold? It is heavy, I know."

"It is," Brightlaw said slowly, "but maybe that's partly

why, Max. The gold he found would give him a spur to keep pushing on. What I wonder is, how in hell did he find it?''

Pulvermacher grinned faintly, wryly. "What man would not wonder? Only the sergeant can say.''

"Right. Just now our concern is how to get him out of here. And ourselves . . .''

Wolf Call made several trips into the brush and back, each time bearing an armful of greasewood. By the time full night-fall had settled, they had a roaring fire going. Its warmth was welcome against the swift cooling of the desert darkness. They had built the fire in a pocketed swale, where its yellow blaze was concealed by the surrounding rises, so as not to lure any enemies. Actually—as Wolf Call observed—it wasn't likely they'd be troubled by hostiles. Desert Indians tended to shun night attacks.

"Ach," Pulvermacher said interestedly. "This has to do with their religion, eh?''

"Mebbeso,'' Wolf Call said taciturnly.

Brightlaw munched distastefully on some pebbly hardtack and jerky, washing it down with a small mouthful of water. Nobody had the taste for cooking up beans or bacon. They were too damned tired to bother, and couldn't afford to waste water on the luxury (if you could call it that) of boiling up Santos coffee.

"Where do we go from here?'' he asked the Cahuilla. "We'll want to cross the freighter road so we can find Lieutenant Umberhine's detail.''

Wolf Call pointed at what seemed to be the northwest, as well as Brightlaw could judge by the constellations in the clear desert sky.

"All right.'' Brightlaw combed the fingers of one hand through his matted hair. "Start out tomorrow, first light. We'll try to travel mostly by night, to escape the heat of day.''

"A good idea,'' Pulvermacher said, then nodded at the unconscious form of Hanrahan. "What about him? He is not dead, yet. How will we carry him?''

"If we got horse, we use travois.'' Wolf Call made vague

motions with his hands. "Hitch 'em onto horse, drag be-hind. But no got horse."

"We can make a litter," Brightlaw said. "Carry it be-tween two of us."

"And the gold?" asked Pulvermacher. "One man it will take to carry just this. But how far can he bear such a load? Or do we leave it here?"

Brightlaw silently debated the question for a moment. "I can't tell yet. Be a hell of an extra burden."

"Maybe anyway we try, *ja*?"

Brightlaw smiled crookedly. "You have a lust for gold, Max?"

"*Nein*. But it is Hanrahan's gold. He wants it a lot or would not carry it so far as this. We can try, *ja*?"

Brightlaw scraped a hand over his whiskered jaw, then nodded. "All right. We can try."

About an hour later Hanrahan groaned his way slowly awake and looked about him, but there was no recognition in his face. His eyes blinked wildly, and perhaps he was lost in the first convulsive throes of fever. Brightlaw laid a hand on his brow. It was burning hot, though the chilling night was rapidly sucking up the day's heat.

Hanrahan groaned and shut his eyes, pulling wind into his mouth in short gasps.

Brightlaw glanced at Wolf Call, then at Pulvermacher. "Well, what can we do? Is there a way to treat that head injury of his?"

"Jimsonweed, mebbeso," Wolf Call said. "I see some around today. But no find any tonight. Wait till morning."

"Max?"

Pulvermacher said wryly, "What can anyone do here? I have no medical supplies. But maybe we move him close to fire, bundle him up in blankets. The fever may sweat out faster then."

"Mmm," Brightlaw murmured. "Well, he'll sweat out plenty tomorrow, if he has anything left to sweat. But we can't just sit here on our butts till his fever breaks. We'll have to move on first light, gentlemen. Meantime we all need some sleep, or we may never move again."

"Water is the big thing, Seth," Pulvermacher said stolidly. "We have what we carry along, but not much is left. A man without food to eat can last maybe a couple weeks. Maybe longer. It has been done. But we will be on the march, carrying all this other stuff. *Ach.* We will weaken quick. Water is the big thing, *ja*? I do not think more than a day or so we can go without water. Maybe not so long as that."

It was a grim prospect any way you sized it.

All they could do for now was to make Hanrahan as comfortable as possible, situating him near the fire. They spread out one blanket under him and piled several more over him, reserving a blanket apiece for themselves.

One man would stay awake. Wolf Call took the first watch.

None of them got more than an hour's sleep apiece. Then the bleak gray light of pre-dawn was on them, and it was time to move again.

Brightlaw and Pulvermacher scoured up two long, fairly straight mesquite poles. They fastened shorter lengths of wood between them to serve as crosspoles, then tied blankets across them to form a litter. Meantime Wolf Call went out and returned shortly with stalks of the tough desert plant called jimsonweed, which—with the aid of a little precious water—he mashed into a poultice that he plastered over Hanrahan's scalp wound and tied fast with a bandanna.

None of it occupied them more than a half hour, and then they distributed their weapons and provisions equally among them. Pulvermacher and Wolf Call lifted Hanrahan onto the litter, then picked up either end of it and began tramping toward the northeast.

Brightlaw trudged along behind them, the blanketful of gold slung across his back. The corners of the blanket were cinched together with a twist of grosgrain ribbon taken from the crown of his black wool Kossuth hat.

Hanrahan revived fitfully from time to time, but mostly he just jogged along on the litter, limp as a dead man. At times he would mutter oaths in English or in obscure phrases of what might have been old-time Gaelic. Brightlaw wondered just how bad his injury was. Surely it hadn't come from just a light blow on the head. Perhaps Hanrahan's skull had been fractured. But even Pulvermacher hadn't been able to determine that for certain.

At first Brightlaw didn't have too much difficulty toting along the weight of gold. As heavy as it was he was in top condition, and just a short rest had strengthened him.

But the gray first light was fading out of the sky, retreating before the first rosy touch of dawn, and soon the sun would be directly in their eyes, the heat of another long desert day steadily increasing.

The men paused often as they went along, resting up in easy but brief stages, conserving their strength for the long miles ahead. Sometimes they would switch places, one or the other taking over the litter duty while the third man took over the gold-toting.

It couldn't go on much longer, Brightlaw was grimly aware. The first after-dawn hours weren't too severe, but the heat was growing steadily. The only solution to their dilemma, as the swelling ache across his back told him, would be to abandon the gold. Maybe to conceal it somewhere and return for it later.

Halfway through the morning they decided to camp in a shadowy swale and catch a little sleep.

As they devoured a handful apiece of their meager rations, Brightlaw said to Wolf Call: "We'll have to leave this damned gold. Put it somewhere that we, or Hanrahan, can find it later."

"Good," grunted the Cahuilla, and pointed with his chin. "You see big mesa over there? I can find it again. We hide gold at the bottom. Okay?"

"Okay." Brightlaw twitched a lip-cracked smile. "Let's do that."

They threw themselves down in the shade and slept through the worst of the blistering midday heat. When they awoke, it was late afternoon. Each took a sip of the waning water. So little of it was left that they were able to pour all of it into a single canteen. And that canteen was now less than half-full.

Also they stuffed their remaining food into a single haversack, then discarded the rifles they had, except for three Winchesters. They kept all the .44 ammunition, along with their pistols. Every ounce of excess gear was left on the spot.

Afterward they ranged over to the big mesa that Wolf Call had pointed out. They dug a shallow trench at the foot of a tall, somewhat isolated spire, and buried the gold there.

Gold, Brightlaw thought with a muddy irony, was the least and last of their concerns now. Men would fight for gold, kill one another for it. They'd been known to lay waste whole kingdoms to obtain it. Yet finally, when it narrowed down to a handful of men faced with the stark option of survival or death, gold meant less than nothing. . . .

CHAPTER FIFTEEN

THE FOLLOWING MORNING THEY LAID UP IN SOME BRUSHY cover as the worst heat of the day quilted the desert.

Hanrahan had fallen into deep fever by then. He babbled of his childhood, his mom and dad, brothers and sisters. Then he was a youth in Boston once more, cursing Protestants so savagely that a man had to wonder what humiliation he had endured at their hands. He also swore up and down against Harvard, that elite school for rich scuts that wouldn't let a Catholic lad even set foot on its sacred precincts.

The men ate a little and drank even less. They had a hellishly long way to go yet, and now they were back in the terrain whose character had been obliterated by the sandstorm. Thus far they had backtracked themselves, but soon they'd be at the point where their own tracks would end in a waste of windswept sand.

Thank God for Wolf Call. He could find their way. But even his lore hadn't been able to locate a source of water, and they couldn't go much farther on what little tepid, almost rancid liquid remained in the canteen.

They still had some uncooked beans and bacon, and a few biscuits, among their provisions. Over a small and almost smokeless fire laid by Wolf Call, they fried up the bacon and packed it away in the haversack. Enough food, altogether, to stretch across maybe another day. They couldn't spare water enough to boil up their fair supply of beans, but did cook up a small amount in the bacon fat. The resultant concoction tasted horrible, but it would lend a man strength, if only he could keep it inside his belly.

Hanrahan's rantings subsided, and he slept. His skin was burning dry, not sweating anymore. That was bad.

None of them was in much better shape. This damned dry, sucking heat! It baked them as dry as dust, shriveling their skins without quite blistering them.

The men caught a few hours' sleep, and that was all they could afford. When they rolled out once more, not long past midday, the coppery sky was still broiling, though now the sun hung to their right and toward their backs. Its fury was hardly dimmed, but at least they weren't facing into it.

Still, the heat drove savagely off a flat desert floor as they crossed it, relieving each other by turns at carrying the litter. The heat danced in crazy shimmers off the barren 'scape, off shining gravel that threw blinding glints, like a sea of marbles.

Again and again Brightlaw had the odd, persistent feeling that he had known this piece of country from some time long ago. Why should that be? He had never been in this section of the Mojave Desert before.

He couldn't explain the conviction. Maybe it stemmed from something he had once read or heard, and then had casually forgotten. That seemed the likeliest explanation.

In any case they wouldn't rest here; the blast of stone-reflected heat was too intense. It rippled up from the earth just as fiercely as it blazed down from above, enough to fry a man to his bowels. If he ever lay down, chances were he would never get up again.

Water . . . water . . . water!

Brightlaw could swear he saw a blue glittering lake of it ahead. He knew the lake was a mirage, yet it was all he could manage to set his teeth against yelling to his companions to get moving, goddammit, there was water just ahead!

The mirage began to fade as they neared it. But beyond, at last, lay a low range of hills. Sand had duned up along its sides, wind-ribbed like the surface of a washboard. And atop the hills flourished plenty of the low-growing greasewood, plus a scant lacing of ocotillo.

They slogged through the deep sand until they reached the top of a dune, and there they collapsed in the meager shade. Each man permitted himself a drink of water. When Brightlaw's turn came, he had to steel himself against bolting down what remained. Afterward he gave the near empty canteen a gentle shake—it sloshed with a few remaining ounces of water.

We're dead, he thought detachedly, almost calmly.

Wolf Call echoed the thought in a grating voice. "No streambed to dig in. I would look for this, but I know the sand has now buried it."

"What about the cactus you tell of?" Pulvermacher said huskily. "The *bisnaga*? It contains water, I am told."

"Yes. Pulp has water. You squeeze it out slow. But I seen no what-you-call-it."

"*Bisnaga*. The barrel cactus, *ja*?"

The Cahuilla grunted. "None around here. We sleep more."

"I done plenty o' that already. . . ."

Hanrahan's voice came out of him as a croaking murmur from deep in his throat.

Just hearing him speak seemed like a miracle. His bearded jaws were parted in a weak but aware grin; his blue eyes were wide open, smiling at them. Good God, the man was a bull. Even under these conditions, his fever had broken; he was holding on tenaciously.

Pulvermacher stirred, heaved himself to his feet, and tramped over to the litter. He hunkered down beside it, slowly shaking his head. "*Mein freund*, any man but you I have met should be now dead."

"Not this 'un, Dutchy."

"I am glad, *Paddy*."

Hanrahan coughed a weak laugh. "Always did appreciate your fine sense of sauerkraut humor, Dutchy." His glance swiveled to Brightlaw, who now squatted down beside the German. "And you, Sassenach. Not sure how glad I should be to see ye. It's clear you got sent to fetch me and my friends."

"You'd be dead if we hadn't, Mike. And the name is Seth. He's Max."

Hanrahan nodded a slow assent. "Good enough. And he"—shuttling a glance at Wolf Call—"is the Delaware. I know."

"You only thought you did. He's a Cahuilla. Born and bred in this country. And he's still Wolf Call by name."

Hanrahan blinked. "Saints. I got some catching up to do. So do you, I reckon. Coyne and O'Flynn, they got fetched by the Mojaves. They—"

"We figured as much. But the Mojaves didn't get you. And you got yourself a good tote-load of gold."

Hanrahan's eyes flared alertly. He heaved himself up on his elbows. "The gold! Aye. Where . . . ?"

"It's not here. But it's safely waiting for you, where we cached it back a ways. Wolf Call can find the place again. Now lie down." Brightlaw smiled faintly. "*I'm* in command of this patrol."

Hanrahan sighed deeply and settled back. "Ye must have done a job of it, bucko. And now we're bound for the fort and a court-martial for Michael Hanrahan. If I'm lucky enough, just be sent to Leavenworth."

There was an awkward silence before Brightlaw said mildly, "Let's concentrate on getting out of here alive. We're in a pretty bad way, Mike. Are you hungry? We have some—"

"*Thirsty*, for God's sake! I doubt I could eat a bite. But we have water? Saints, I could drink an ocean dry!"

Brightlaw and Pulvermacher exchanged glances, and then Max sighed and got up wearily and brought the canteen over, handing it to the Irishman.

Hanrahan had guessed the truth from their expressions. It showed on his face as he gave the canteen one quick shake. "That's all?"

"I'm afraid so, Mike," Brightlaw said.

"To Sheol with it, then." Hanrahan tried to thrust the

canteen aside, but Brightlaw grabbed it and said flatly, "You drink. We're all at the end of our string."

"But I'll be damned if I'll drink the last of your water!"

"It's *our* water. Drink it."

"Hell, I'm as good as dead, anyway!"

"No. You're not dead yet. You've got the guts to dog it out, Irish, if any of us has. Are you a believer?"

"In what?"

"I don't know," Brightlaw said quietly. "In Providence, maybe. I've never been too religious myself. But we'll all get out of this damned desert, or none of us will. If we don't trust to Providence . . . there's nothing else."

Hanrahan groaned softly. "Aye . . . aye, then. Give me the water, Seth."

Hanrahan finished off the canteen. Then he demanded to be caught up on what had happened after he'd passed out.

It was a time for honesty. Brightlaw told him everything, including the details of his longtime feud with Lieutenant Umberhine and what had landed him and Pulvermacher and Wolf Call in this situation. And about the death of Idaho Bitters.

"Ah," murmured Hanrahan. "There's a pity. He died as senselessly as my two lads did. If there's any sense at all to any of it."

"Damned if I know," Brightlaw said. "But we have to *believe* there is, even so. It's all that keeps us going. We're made that way."

"Aye. Even if our beliefs divide us in bitter wars. What d'ye think, Max?"

Pulvermacher shrugged. "I never know. *Deutschland*, Germany you people call it, sure divided is. From Bavaria I come, and there Catholics rule. In our good neighbor Prussia, the Protestants, they run everything. Who is to say who is in the right? Yet they kill each other over little differences. And all of them hate the Jews. Who is right? Is anyone right?"

Hanrahan's lips stretched in a brittle effort at a grin. "You

know? Between ye, you lads have given me more food for
thought than I've known in a lifetime. . . . ''

His eyes were faintly glazed; he was staring into the hot,
brassy sky above. What he plainly needed was more sleep.
They all did.

Brightlaw was curious about the source of the gold, but
there would be time later to query Hanrahan on that matter.
If they stayed alive long enough . . .

"We'd all best catch some sleep," Brightlaw said. "We'll
be on the march again about sunset.''

When they were on the move once more, the sun hung
low at their backs, like a fuzzy, swollen orange with a flam-
ing penumbra of light around it. From the horizon ahead the
darkness of night was flowing up, a slow seep of blue deepening into purple as the sky took on the color of coming
night.

They trudged slowly, bearing Hanrahan on the litter. He
had sunk into a deep torpor, but very likely his powerful
constitution would throw off his remaining weakness . . . *if
only they had water*! Even the slow drain of coolness into
nightfall couldn't begin to offset the lack of water.

Again they moved along carefully, in easy stages, pausing
often to rest. They were all weakening fast, and within hours
they would be at the end of their tether. Only the blind instinct to live impelled them onward.

They had no difficulty finding their way, however. Wolf
Call, whether he was toting the front end of the litter, or just
tramping ahead of them, always had a sure sense of direction.
Mainly—as he reaffirmed to Brightlaw—it was just a matter
of singling out particular landmarks that he had known even
as a child. These were the black towering cinder cones of the
ancient volcanoes that had erupted into being so many centuries ago.

Again Brightlaw felt assaulted by an overpowering sense
of familiarity. Why did he keep feeling that this land had
existed in his distant past, even though he had never been in
the region before?

As the sun's last ruddy rays dissolved into twilight and then dusk, Brightlaw had some difficulty in distinguishing objects of the landscape. But with the coming of full night, that handicap was gone. It was a night typical of the southwestern desert. Everything stood out with a crystalline purity under the stars, an unreal beauty of silver sheens and black shadows.

Again Brightlaw felt a sense of awe. The whole universe was so vast, so unknown. Men were nothing more than ants crawling across the scarred face of the Mojave. Its stark clarity seemed to etch itself on his eyeballs.

All three of the men were just about used up. Brightlaw called a halt, aware from his own weak, stumbling movements that this might be their last stop. He was dizzy, and his muscles ached to the bone. His skin was cold from the night's chill, cold to the touch, even as his brain seemed to burn with real or imagined fever.

"All right, gentlemen," he heard himself say. "Let's bed down awhile. A few hours' sleep . . ."

Nobody said a word. All of them were so dog-tired they were ready to drop in their tracks.

Brightlaw slept the sleep of a dead man. He had no dreams at all. Finally he felt a hand on his shoulder, roughly shaking him awake. Wolf Call had taken the first watch. Now, crouching beside Seth, he motioned that it was his turn.

Brightlaw crawled groggily to his feet. He settled himself on his haunches at the edge of their small camp, rifle across his knees, yawning, fighting to keep awake. Sooner or later, he thought, I'll just go under. And that'll be the end.

At first, when the terrific clarity of the desert night began to dim in his sight, he thought that exactly this was happening. Everything was blurring around the edges, and part of his consciousness seemed to be slipping away.

A chuckle of irony rasped in his throat. *Good-bye, cruel world.* He was sure that he was dying. Then, suddenly, he was no longer sure.

All the landscape around him seemed cloaked in a peculiar

haze. On a lank dune of sand not a hundred feet away stood the figure of a woman.

She was so dimly seen that he could barely perceive her outline. Yet he sensed that it was the form of a woman, slender and young.

She stood erect on the dune, a faintly glowing figure, one arm flung out from her side. She was pointing with an extended arm in a direction almost due north.

There. She was directing him toward something.

I don't understand, Brightlaw thought. There's *what*?

Water, the figure seemed to answer.

Water? How far away?

Not far. Go that way, and you will find it.

Who are you? What are you?

Even as the words framed themselves in his mind she was vanishing in his eyes, fading slowly and gradually away.

And she was gone.

CHAPTER SIXTEEN

ALMOST AT ONCE THE DIM, OBSCURE LOOK OF THE DESERT night, the landscape around, swam back into focus.

Brightlaw sprang to his feet, his hands clenched into fists. He was shaking all over, and he would have been sweating if he'd had enough body water left to sweat.

What had that image of a woman been? Had he been plunged into an hallucination born of his own thirst and exhaustion, his fevered state of mind?

I don't believe it, he thought, but couldn't explain why. He had been fully awake, no matter how badly his brain was functioning. On that level all of it had savored of a strange reality.

She had been standing there, and somehow she had communicated with him, linking her thoughts to his without spoken words.

A weakness seized Brightlaw's muscles; he sank down on his haunches again. I have to keep the watch, he thought doggedly. A sudden drowsiness seized him, and he had to fight against it as he crouched under the icy starlight.

Was there really water nearby? They'd have to wait until first light to find out. And the longer he squatted where he was, trying to fight back the drowsy feeling that kept assailing him, the more overpowering the anxiety became. *I have to know.*

Hallucination or reality . . . he had to verify or disprove it to his own mind. What other choice was there? Without water they would all be done for in a few more hours. So he'd have to wait until first light had dispelled enough of the darkness for them to make a search.

North. She had pointed north. . . .

He came awake with a sudden shock as Pulvermacher touched his shoulder and said in a mildly reproving voice, "Seth. You went to sleep. For my watch it is time."

It was still full dark. Brightlaw stumbled back to his blanket and dropped into a space of dreamless sleep.

When he woke again, his brain was clear. The gray light of pre-dawn was edging up from the east. Light enough to see by.

Max was bleary-eyed and Wolf Call was alert, although expressionless, as Brightlaw told them of his strange vision of a dream girl, whoever or whatever she'd been. He spoke slowly and carefully, admitting his own self-doubts. He didn't want either man to think that a semi-delirious man was in charge of this patrol.

Hanrahan came weakly awake as Seth was talking and he didn't interrupt, only peered intently at Brightlaw.

"That's it," Brightlaw said finally, wearily. "She said there was water not far away."

"But to the north, *ja*?" Pulvermacher stroked his chin, speculatively. "If we go that way, we go off our route, which is northwest."

"That's right." Brightlaw glanced at the Cahuilla. "What do you think?"

Wolf Call, settled on his heels with his arms crossed on his knees, gave the slightest of shrugs. "Not know. But see strange things on desert sometime. Maybe we go look. We out of water anyhow, eh?"

"Yes. Max, you stay with Michael, and Wolf Call and I will scout over north. If we don't find anything, we'll be back shortly. . . ."

They didn't have to look any farther than over the next rise. They found it less than a hundred yards from their camp: a natural bowl formed out of the weathered rock. Located in the lee of a huge formation, it had been sheltered from any strong blasts of wind and sand.

The bottom of the basin was half-filled with sand, but above it lay at least two feet of pure water, trapped by old rains and now sand-filtered. Plentiful water, glistening under the shine of gray light, and it looked good to drink.

Both Brightlaw and Wolf Call lay on their bellies and drank, cupping the water to their mouths with their hands, swallowing it in deep gulps.

"Not too much at first," the Cahuilla cautioned, and then raised his head, grinning a little. "That woman you see. I think she comes from *Teimkesh*."

"From . . . what?"

"*Teimkesh*." Wolf Call paused. "Not know what you white-eyes call it. We Cahuilla call it 'Land of the Dead.' "

Brightlaw paused in the act of splashing more water across his head and back, feeling his parched flesh revive. "Land of the Dead," he echoed, his voice sinking to a whisper. "Good Christ. But why . . . how?"

"Not know. But sometime things happen. I hear talk from people who live here long ago. Old people of my tribe."

Brightlaw nodded. "Oh . . . I see. By way of oral tradition, eh?"

"Not know how you call it." Again Wolf Call paused. "We got words for it you not know. Maybe . . . from Other Side."

"Ah." Brightlaw rose slowly to his feet. "Part of the lore of your people? Well, I can't argue that much. Here's the water."

"Unh," grunted the Cahuilla.

Brightlaw gnawed his underlip, shaking his head puzzledly. "But . . . who the hell *was* she? Why did she appear to *me*? Was there some reason?"

"Mebbeso."

Knowing from that terse, characteristic response that he wasn't likely to get any more out of Wolf Call now, Brightlaw said, "All right. Let's get some of this water into our friends."

* * *

Brightlaw had brought along their one canteen. He filled it and carried it back to camp. He let Hanrahan drink a measured amount, and then Pulvermacher drained most of the rest, too thirsty to pay attention to Wolf Call's warning not to take too much. The big German drank his fill, then poured the rest of the water over his head, grinning hugely.

He and Brightlaw made more trips back to the rock-basined tank, each time bringing back a canteen full of water. Brightlaw regretted now that they had discarded their other canteens. But at least they could lie here for a brief spell while they luxuriated in getting their strength back.

They drank all the water they wanted, then poured it over their heads and bodies, literally soaking in it.

Before noonday they all felt restored enough to move across the rise and into the rocky shelter above the basin, toting Hanrahan's litter with them.

With the water, the Irishman had picked up incredibly. The usual ruddy tinge had flowed back into his broad face. He sat up on his litter, taking a little water from time to time, regaling his companions with cheery observations.

"I'll tell ye, Seth," he said. "I'm inclined to believe there's something to it all. The lady you seen on the mound yonder, and what she told ye."

"You think so?"

"Aye. The water was there, wasn't it? Maybe it's the Celtic in me. A streak of . . . eh . . . the mystic. Me ancestors believed in it absolutely, and in the Little People, the Wee Folk, and so on. Could be you have a spot of it in your own ancestry, bucko."

"Lord forbid," Brightlaw said good-humoredly.

Hanrahan threw back his head, letting out a feeble bray of laughter. "Aye, doubt it if you will! But if you've any better way of explaining the matter, tell me what it is."

Brightlaw shook his head. "I don't have any."

With water available, they were able to cook up their supply of beans. They boiled it to a slushy consistency that was at least edible. It would stretch out, along with their remaining provisions, for a day or so longer. Wolf Call found some more jimsonweed close by and mashed it up so that he could change Hanrahan's poultice.

When late afternoon drew on, they took up the trek eastward once more. They moved with slow but swinging strides, undeterred by the relentless press of the Mojave sun. It was as though they all felt somehow renewed, felt an inner assurance that they would make it through after all.

It was close to nightfall when Hanrahan said abruptly, "All right, buckoes. Set down the litter."

Brightlaw and Pulvermacher were bearing him, both feeling a terrible ache in their muscles by now. They hesitated, and then Brightlaw nodded when Max gave him a questioning glance. They lowered the litter to the ground.

Hanrahan eased himself slowly to his feet, staggered a little, and braced his feet under him. "That'll be enough of it," he told them. "I'll make me own way now."

Seth was doubtful that Hanrahan could manage to do so, but he did. He plodded along slowly and doggedly, his head bent downward, but keeping pace with them. When Brightlaw called another halt as full darkness settled, Hanrahan was glad to settle down and partake of their food supply. It was the first grub he'd eaten in some time, and he ate as heartily as he was able to.

They talked as they ate, Hanrahan telling of his own experiences down to the last detail: how Coyne and O'Flynn had died, the dead conquistador, the discovery of the gold.

"That is really something," Pulvermacher observed, taking a small swig of water from the canteen. "The remains of an old Spanish conquistador, eh? And there you find the gold."

"That's how it was, Dutch—eh, Max. If you can spell out better'n I did how the chap come to be there, I'd admire to hear it."

"I cannot. But the gold, it will be yours. We will see to that. Nobody else will we tell. When the time comes, Wolf Call will find it for you."

The Cahuilla grunted an assent.

Hanrahan scowled. He rubbed a hand over his whiskers, looking somewhat sheepish. He muttered, "Ahhh . . ." then looked straight at each of them in turn. "All right. Done. But I want to say this. All of us, we four . . . we'll share equally in the damned gold."

"No need for—" Brightlaw began, but Hanrahan cut him off roughly.

"That's how it'll be. Damned if I ever thought I'd feel such a kinship with a Sassenach, a sauerkraut man, and an Injun! But I do. The fates or the saints or whatever have flung us here together, I believe, for a reason . . . for a meaning. And we'll share whatever comes of it all."

Brightlaw held a lingering suspicion of Hanrahan's generous declaration. It might be a subterfuge, one designed to relax their guard and enable Hanrahan to escape them—and whatever punishment he might have to endure as a deserter.

So Brightlaw took the first watch, after Wolf Call and Pulvermacher had settled down for sleep. Then he talked with Hanrahan, who was looking more alert by the hour, as they squatted on either side of a small fire.

They conversed in friendly generalities for a while. Then Brightlaw said bluntly, "Mike, what was it with you and us Bostonians? How did you come to hate us as much as you do? I know you must have had strong reasons to start with. . . ."

Hanrahan sighed. "But there must have been more to it?"

"Yes."

"I'll tell ye, Seth. Picture an Irish lad, little more than an infant, brought over from Ireland by his dad and mum. Picture him being thrust into a Protestant school, and the disdainful treatment of him every day by his teachers and nearly all his fellow students. Picture him seeing his own father treated like dirt by his employers, year after year."

"What did your father do for a living?"

"Drove a dray. He had the duty of carting goods from the railroad depot, stuff that was shipped to his several employers' stores. The American-born did that, too, but they were never treated like shit.''

"And you?'' Brightlaw asked.

"No better. Worse. Attending what you American-born call public schools, I was compelled to recite a Protestant prayer every day. It went contrary to all me early learning. Every day I defied them. And every day I got a savage whipping from the headmaster.''

"Lord," Brightlaw murmured. "I didn't know. . . .''

"Doubtless ye attended all-Protestant public schools. But every day I got whipped. This for a whole month. And then I give in. I meekly followed their damned rules, vowing that when I got out of school I'd be me own man, no matter what the cost.''

Brightlaw could imagine how a man of Hanrahan's pride must have felt. "But it didn't work that way?''

"Need ye ask? I got work with the same Sassenachs who employed my father. They heaped insults on me that my dad could bear but I couldn't. One day I smashed one of the bastards in the face and then walked off the job. That same day I went to the recruiting office and enlisted in the army. But the memory of them schoolboy floggings and the rest of it . . . they never left me.''

After catching a few hours' sleep apiece, they set out once more. A gloss of star-sheen picked out their way as clear as daylight.

As early dawn was fading, they were pretty well tuckered. Brightlaw was about to signal a halt when Wolf Call said huskily, "There. See road? Where your pony soldiers go by.''

The others couldn't yet make out the landscape that clearly. But before they had covered another hundred yards, the trampled trace of the road showed plainly in the growing light.

CHAPTER SEVENTEEN

THEY REACHED THE ROAD AND SWUNG SOUTH ALONG IT, following the near fresh prints of Umberhine's patrol. The going was a lot easier now, for they had passed beyond the eastern perimeter of the swath cut by the sandstorm and the road surface was firm, ordinarily being well traveled by both wagons and horsemen.

However, they came on disquieting evidence that Umberhine's patrol had run into trouble. At one place they found a litter of spent cartridge cases where the troopers had been forced to defend themselves.

From what Wolf Call could tell, the troop had been surprised by a band of Mojave raiders. He could read the sign plainly. No Mojave dead were to be found, of course, but the troop had suffered several casualties, as the mounded graves offside the road showed.

"Small bunch Mojave," Wolf Call said. "Pony soldiers drive 'em off. But it look like all the Mojave; they are, what you say, out in force."

"Out for blood," Brightlaw said soberly. "Ours, too, if we run into any."

"Unh. Go slow. We rest soon. Be near San Bernardino tomorrow, mebbeso."

If so, the rest of their troop must be there by now.

True to his sense of duty, Brightlaw admitted that he wanted to be with his fellow troopers, up ahead where the action would be. Pulvermacher, in spite of his pacifist tendencies, confessed the same feeling. These were their com-

rades who might be in deep trouble by now, and no man with
an ounce of guts in his craw would want to be left out. . . .

But the Cahuilla was right. The sun was getting high, and
the last coolness was fading from the 'scape. A stiff wind
was blowing straight at them, and dust devils were starting
to dance on a scatter of playas, the beds of dry lakes that
glared whitely under the sun, crusted with alkali and salts of
various kinds. When the sun began to pour down more savagely, heat waves would distort the appearance and distance
of nearly everything.

They came on a dry streambed that crossed the road. Here,
Wolf Call thought, there might be water. They could dig for
it. Welcome news, with the last moisture in their single canteen almost gone.

They tramped down the streambed. Where Wolf Call
pointed, beneath an overhang of shrubbery, they dug. The
water was there, under dust-dry sand that turned suddenly
moist beneath their scrabbling fingers. They dug out a wide,
deep basin, then waited for the water to fill it slowly.

Taking their time, they drank all they wanted and refilled
the canteen. The water wasn't the purest they'd ever tasted,
but Wolf Call pronounced it good enough. Then they ate
sparingly of their cooked provisions, munching them down
in slow gulps with small swallows of water.

We're not sure how far we have to go, Brightlaw thought
as he ate. The distance was hard to nail down using the
Cahuilla's sense of time passing. The white man's measures
of time and miles meant little to him.

Even though he was outnumbered and unarmed, Michael
Hanrahan, at least, looked in fine fettle, sauntering along at
their sides. Still, he looked more grim than cheerful, and
he'd said practically nothing more since his private words to
Brightlaw last night. After all, Hanrahan was going back to
face desertion charges.

Despite his sympathy for the Irishman, Brightlaw had no
intention of letting him slip away before he was delivered
into Umberhine's custody.

Some sandstone outcrops not far from the road provided

good shade and they laid up there, taking the usual three-men watch. . . .

Brightlaw awoke to Wolf Call's grip on his shoulder. The Cahuilla said nothing, just pointed toward the road. Brightlaw listened intently.

Horsemen were coming slowly through the noonday heat. He could faintly pick out the thud of horses' hooves, the drift of men's voices. In an Indian dialect?

Their own party could not be seen from the road, and Wolf Call wordlessly motioned that Brightlaw should awaken the others. He did, and then softly apprised them of what they would probably have to face. The men took up positions behind the outcrop, careful not to show themselves.

They heard the sound of riders halting on the road. The warriors' voices rose to excited gabblings. They had spotted the tracks where four men had left the road, following the streambed. From the sound they were following the tracks slowly, not talking now but still mounted, their ponies shuffling softly along the dry streambed. Soon they would discover where the troopers had halted to dig. . . .

"Hai!" Brightlaw heard one of them murmur softly and sharply.

The Mojaves had found where the tracks branched off toward the outcrop. Brightlaw edged one eye out around a jag of rock.

There were twelve of them. The leader had lifted his rifle above his head, swinging it toward the shallow incline that led upward toward the sheltering rocks.

"Now," Brightlaw murmured between his teeth, "before they can come on . . . *let 'em have it!*"

The first volley took four Indians hard and fast, rolling them out of their saddles. The rest, demoralized, dropped to their ponies and scattered for cover.

The exchange of gunfire kept up for about a half hour.

The Mojaves, foiled in their attempt to take the enemy by

surprise, were stubbornly furious. They returned a steady answering fire.

Wolf Call was wounded. Not by a direct hit. A bullet had ricocheted off a rock slab behind him, and he'd grunted and then sagged down on his face.

Hanrahan was at his side at once, rolling him on his back, ripping open his shirt, examining the exit wound of the bullet.

"It's a bad one," he muttered. "But not a fatal one, I'm thinking. See, the slug ranged from above his left shoulder blade and come out above his heart and lungs. . . ."

Brightlaw turned his sweating face away from the pounding roar of gunfire, the stink of cordite. "But what in hell can we do for him?"

Pulvermacher had started to swing away from his position, but Hanrahan said, "We'll see. No, Max, stick to your post; I can fix him up for now as well as need be. Keep your attention on the red divils."

Hanrahan made compresses and prepared a bandage torn from Wolf Call's own shirt to circle the Cahuilla's barrel chest. Wolf Call had been knocked unconscious with shock, but he groaned and tried to heave himself upright as Hanrahan finished tying off the bandage.

"Not now, me man, you lay back," Hanrahan said gently. "I'll take over your rifle. If Private Brightlaw has got no objection. Ye'll need all the gun power you can muster, Seth."

Brightlaw hesitated only a moment. "All right. But I want your word."

"Not to try a break while I have his rifle in my hands?"

"Yes."

"Ye've got it, bucko."

"You're still going back to stand trial . . . if we get out of this alive."

"Aye. Ye've my word on that, too."

Brightlaw met Hanrahan's steady gaze, hesitated again, and then nodded. There was a half-spoken bond between them, and their party would need all the "gun power" they could get—for this situation, and maybe more to come.

Nevertheless, Brightlaw felt obliged to add, "I can testify on your behalf, Mike, when it comes to that. It might help."

"Aye." Hanrahan showed the crooked edge of a smile. "Who knows? It might."

He moved up between Brightlaw and Pulvermacher and opened fire. He was a prime hand as a sharpshooter, even with the unfamiliar Winchester, and maybe this was what helped turn things in their favor.

They inflicted wounds on two more Mojaves. Abruptly the hostiles decided to quit the fight. Their leader was still unscathed, and now he shouted an order at his fellows. Almost as one they ducked out of cover and, bending their bodies in low crouches, ran out to recover their dead or wounded, as well as their straying ponies.

"Hold your fire!" Brightlaw shouted. "They've given up . . . let 'em go."

Wolf Call had been seriously hit, but he was a proud and stubborn man. With Pulvermacher's help, he re-dressed his own wounds at back and front, using poultices of the jimsonweed in which he placed such great trust, perhaps justifiably.

"I go on with you," he told his companions. "We find Umberhine pretty soon all right."

After resting through the worst of the day's heat, they continued along the road, marching slowly in deference to Hanrahan's and Wolf Call's injuries.

The Irishman was holding up well, but the Cahuilla plodded slowly, his chin sunk almost on his chest. Twice he stumbled and fell, and had to be helped to his feet. As tough as he was, he couldn't keep up with them much longer.

Even more ominous, they came up against the dawning realization of another handicap. As they moved southwest along the San Bernardino road, they found its formerly well-defined arc gradually fading into nothingness. The sandstorm had swept this far south, erasing the southernmost traces of horse and wagon traffic.

Damn! Brightlaw thought with a mounting despair. None of them except Wolf Call had ever covered this terrain before. The Cahuilla was groggy, lurching on his feet, and his desert-bred senses were dulled.

"I no good no more," he said finally, stoically. "I only hold you back. Leave me. Go on."

"We can leave some food with you. But water . . ."

"There water close by." The Cahuilla waved a hand, feebly, toward the rolling desert 'scape. "I sure of that much. I find it if I live. I not live, I go to *Teimkesh*. We all go there at last. You white-eyes, too."

No use to argue the matter. Wolf Call had the stoic fatalism of his race, his upbringing.

They found the shelter of some rocks, laced around with scanty greasewood, and settled him down in his blanket, giving him generous draughts of water from the canteen.

Brightlaw felt as guilty as hell. This wasn't right. Nor could he really explain what was driving him onward. A sense of duty? Sure. But somehow the feeling ran deeper. Like a sense of *destiny*.

Considered from any rational view it seemed foolish enough, but there it was again. The overriding sense that he had known this land from sometime before . . . from long ago.

"Teimkesh," he said quietly, bending above Wolf Call. "What it is? Can you tell me?"

The Cahuilla stirred his head once from side to side, his eyes shining and feverish under the fading sunlight. "You white-eyes, you not know. It is the Other Side. Not know how say it. You go on now."

They left him there and resumed the slow trek.

As well as he was able, Wolf Call had pointed out the way they should take, via the constellations now forming in the clear evening sky. But it seemed a highly generalized direction. How far could they follow it and hope to arrive at their destination?

That question became more urgent as they tramped along. The stars were fading from the sky, drowned in an obscure gray light that wiped out all sense of direction except for the slow pink of coming dawn in the east.

The three troopers all felt the same drowsy drag in their senses, their muscles. They could no longer guide themselves by the constellations, and they were dead weary. Without Wolf Call's guidance they were in damned serious straits.

"We have to rest," Brightlaw said. "We have to sleep. . . ."

Exhaustedly, they bedded down where they were, near the flank of a tall dune.

Again Brightlaw had an illusory vision. Sitting his guard watch, he began to drowse off. Then he dimly awoke to a hazy impression of the ghostly young woman.

She was standing atop the dune, and again a misty glow seemed to surround her. This time she was limned more clearly in his sight. But as before her arm was flung straight out from her side.

You go that way.

What are you? Brightlaw asked back, feeling the same psychic union with her as he had before.

I knew you a long time ago. We are as one, you and I.

I don't understand! He tried to yell the thought back at her.

There are many lives. You and I have lived them before. Here and in other places.

You are from . . . the Other Side? Brightlaw asked silently.

Among the Old Ones, yes. I am there now. There is no death. There is only change. You were born again. I was not. I do not know why. But sometime we will be together again. Go the way I show you. You will find those you seek. . . .

He thought he sensed a smile on her face. But even as she spoke the woman's form was slowly vanishing, fading gently away as a fog might. Brightlaw flung out a hand, as if by doing so he could grasp her, prevent her from disappearing.

But again she was gone.

CHAPTER EIGHTEEN

STRETCHED ON HIS BACK, WOLF CALL DOZED FOR A TIME. He never really slept. Sometimes, slowly and gropingly, he would come half-awake, aware of how hot and parched his flesh was. Then he would slide back to the edge of oblivion.

The night was dwindling to paleness in the east when he finally grasped enough of a hold on consciousness to realize that dawn, and the onslaught of a new flaming-hot day, was almost on him.

Wolf Call tried to stir and felt the blaze of pain ripple through his upper body. He managed to hitch himself up slowly, inch by inch, along the rugged surface of a boulder until he was in a sitting position, his back against it.

For a while he sat gasping, hauling in deep breaths, his head tipped back against the rock. If as little as this dragged-out effort could leave him so spent, could he muster the strength to do more?

Perhaps *Teimkesh* is very close now, he thought.

The agony of the wound was excruciating, but he must master it and move from this place somehow. Or die where he was.

Wolf Call was no longer young. He had lived through fifty summers and more. Also, he had a deeply ingrained fatalism. He did not know whether a man could expect any life after death or not. He had lived long enough to know that all men were prey to such uncertainties, whatever they might profess to believe. But the will to live, to somehow survive in the here and now, was blind and unthinking.

From his long association with white men Wolf Call knew that they felt there was no real significance to the Indians' religion. An Indian would pray to the sun, the moon, the stars, the wind, or the lightning. He felt that cosmic forces were beyond man's real understanding, and so he would symbolize them in terms of observable phenomena.

He knew of the white-eyes' idea that there was a particular God, modeled after their own conception of themselves, except that it was enlarged into a particular Being that, whoever it might be, resided in a particular place that somehow dominated the universe. Indians might be willing to concede that much, but they would argue that if it were so, there must be an unmistakable road that would lead to that place.

Further, Indians believed that if there was a physical place in the hereafter for spirits of the good, they should bury with the dead person his or her favorite bridle and saddle and beads and cooking utensils and other personal possessions. When the man or woman was dead, they would split in half everything that had belonged to him or her in life, and one half would be placed over the corpse, to provide him or her with a helpful passage into the afterlife.

They believed that spirits of evil people would be resurrected on earth in the forms of coyotes or bears or cougars or snakes, which was the reason Indians tried to avoid killing any of those animals. Or . . . they might cross to the Other Side and be with the Old Ones.

Wolf Call was too old and too skeptical to trust in the absolute truth of any such beliefs. But he was not so sure that all of them were untrue.

He thought of the image of a woman that Brightlaw believed he had seen. Though Brightlaw was a white-eyes, he seemed to have come upon some revelation from the Other Side. And whether by design or by accident, it had guided him to water.

Somehow the remembrance sent a shudder of determination through the Cahuilla. He steeled himself against the awareness of pain, against the overriding, mind-numbing agony of it, and began to inch himself to his feet.

His back scraped along the boulder as he used it for a support, and the pain almost caused him to pass out. He managed to straighten his legs beneath him so that they would bear his weight.

Once on his feet, Wolf Call was dimly surprised by the discovery that he could actually stand upright. The very act of rising had lent him a thrust of strength.

He took a cautious step away from the boulder. He tottered. For a moment he thought he would fall down again. But he didn't. Putting all his will into the effort he took a step forward, and then another, and found he could stand alone.

If *Teimkesh* awaited him, so it would be. But a man would strive to live as long as the will to live remained strong in him. If he let go his grasp of that will, he deserved to die.

I am a man and a Cahuilla. I am not ready for the Land of the Dead.

By keeping his legs stiff and straight beneath him, not permitting his knees to hinge, he found that he could take one plodding step after another.

As always, water was the big consideration. Wolf Call was fairly sure he could find some not far away. He did not have an occult premonition such as those Brightlaw seemed to have, but he had a lifelong familiarity with this terrain. Its prominent landmarks, as well as his general knowledge of the desert, could still guide him. He felt an instinctive sureness of it.

He inspected his meager gear. There was little that he actually needed, and he couldn't afford to burden himself unnecessarily. His Winchester was leaning against the boulder he had quitted, and he knew it still contained a few shells.

Fastened to his belt was a short length of horse intestine, tied off at both ends, that he had taken from the body of one of the Mojaves they had downed. It now contained only a little vile-tasting water, but in his time he had subsisted on worse. Probably no white-eyes' stomach could keep it down. By his standards they were an incredibly fastidious people.

Moving very slowly and carefully, Wolf Call gathered up his blanket and rifle. He turned his head in a half circle, scanning the landscape. The day was still young, not unbearably hot yet, and he could see the landmarks clearly enough. Heat distortion had not begun to affect his vision, and his head was clearer than it had been.

Maybe the pain helped. Lancing from the back to the front of his body, it prodded him to a high awareness. He felt somewhat rested. But it was only a false, brief strength, he knew. The blasting heat of another desert day would soon sap that strength, and he must find water before then.

A man could go for a surprising time without food, and he wanted no food just now. *Water* was all of it.

He took his bearings from the ancient formations and then, unhesitating, pushed along due north. The sandstorm, as severe as any he had encountered in all his years, might have wiped out all immediately familiar signs, but it could not dull the perceptions of a whole lifetime.

Still Wolf Call lost track of passing time as he forged along, occasionally resting his back against a projection of rock. He wouldn't take the risk of sitting down again, knowing what an ordeal it would be to get back on his feet.

Only the steady rising of the sun and its increasing warmth lent him a sense of urgency. All the land he had known was wind-scourged, changed by shifting sands.

Finally he saw it—a lone jimsonweed protruding above the desert floor. For all its toughness the jimsonweed needed moisture. It was not so sure a sign of available water as the smoke trees were, but it was a place that would bear examination.

Wolf Call eased himself down a shallow swale and was briefly cut off from view of the jimson. Then he drove himself up the far slope and came to a dead halt.

A short distance from him stood the wounded Mojave from their first gunfight. Not standing so much as half crawling, still using his rifle as a crutch.

If Wolf Call were a white-eyes, he might have felt a biting sense of irony. (He knew from observing the whites that they had such feelings, though he was too inherently fatalistic to

see any sense to it.) This was the same Mojave warrior that
Brightlaw had prevented him from killing miles back. The
dirty red bandanna tied around his head identified him. Wolf
Call had warned Brightlaw that he might be sorry for sparing
him, yet it was he, not Brightlaw, who was now confronted
with the enemy.

Both of them came to a stop.

Wolf Call could see the straggling line of the Mojave's
back trail, looping this way and that, one leg pulling him
along while the other dragged uselessly behind him. He was
still gripping his rifle, crutching along on it, and only the
gods knew what iron tenacity had brought him this far, even
if his sense of direction was aimless and uncertain.

His eyes wore a dull varnish of fever, and he must be
nearly out of his head. The eyes held an awareness of the
Cahuilla's presence, but no glint of recognition. Only a dim
awareness that he faced an enemy.

He gave a racking cough and tried to lift his rifle. That
single effort caused him to collapse, falling on his face.
Somehow he heaved himself over on his back, trying again
to lift the weapon and failing. He had lost much blood, as
the whole crimson-soaked side of one leg showed.

Wolf Call made his way laboriously over to the man and
stood above him. It would be easy to kill him.

Yet he had no wish to kill. They were two fellow creatures
striving to live. Only that thought filled his mind now.

"You are hurt to death," Wolf Call said in the Mojave
dialect.

The other flickered his eyelids. "You are Cahuilla, I
think," he whispered. "What do you care?"

"I do not know. I remembered this place from before the
winds blew. Maybe there is water."

"I do not remember. I think maybe so. Do you want to
kill me?"

"You are hurt to death," Wolf Call repeated. "I do not
think so."

The Mojave's eyes closed and a deep sigh of out-rushing
breath left him.

Soon he will be dead, Wolf Call thought. Mebbeso me, too. He took the rifle from the Mojave's limp hands and cast it safely aside.

The jimsonweed poultice he wore was a rancid mess by now. It had checked his bleeding but was doing him no more good; he should change it. He let himself down on his rump to the ground, macerated a chunk of the fresh jimsonweed between his palms, and added a little more water from his horse-gut canteen. Then, fighting back the waves of dizzy sickness that again threatened to engulf him, he removed the bandages that Pulvermacher had bound around his wounds and cleaned the old mess of poultice away as well as he could, plastering the wounds with the fresh mixture. He re-wrapped the stained bandages around them.

From time to time Wolf Call glanced at the unconscious Mojave, not sure what he should feel. The man was an enemy. Nearly all men outside the bands of his own tribe were enemies. Even his alliance with the white-eyes was a tenuous thing, born of the need for survival in the white-eyes' world.

The white-eyes were never satisfied with the ways of old, the ways that had prevailed for ages. They had to change everything, everything that men had always known. He did not hate or blame them. What they were, they were. But he, too, had had to change in order to live. Wolf Call would not sit in a brush hogan wrapped in his blanket as did other aging men of his tribe, clustered in their lonely enclaves.

To live, a man must act. Or he was not alive at all.

Wolf Call began to dig with his hands. Often he rested, always fighting back the urge to let his will and consciousness trail away. Below the roots of the jimson there must be moisture. If he could find enough of it, he would live. He would make himself live.

Yes . . . there was moisture. He dug deeper, his teeth gritted. He would have to dig a ways further.

Again he heard the Mojave's heavy rush of breath, and he looked at him. The man was absolutely motionless now. His eyes were open, but they stared at nothing at all.

I am sorry, Wolf Call thought. My enemy . . . my brother.

CHAPTER NINETEEN

Afterwards HIS SECOND VISITATION BY THE GHOSTLY INDIAN, Brightlaw was alert once more. He didn't doze off again. He was relieved of his guard watch by Pulvermacher and Hanrahan, in their turns.

When these were finished, it was nearly dawn. They had enough light to see by, and they continued on southeast.

Brightlaw couldn't have explained why, but now he was certain that he was on the right track. They were still isolated on an unrecognizable terrain in one of the most barren regions on the earth, they had no trail to follow, yet Brightlaw was sure that he was going in the right direction. He felt an inward *sureness* about it.

As before, they paused often in easy stages to rest. At their first stop Brightlaw told the other two about his most recent visitation from the spectral Indian girl.

Hanrahan shook his head.

"I dunno, Seth. I can't give ye a likely answer. There are things of which we know nothing, so we have the old legends to explain them."

Pulvermacher had a more scientific turn of mind. He was eager to elaborate on his thoughts. "Seth, you have heard of Pythagoras?"

"Yes. Of course." Brightlaw rubbed a hand tiredly over his jaw. "I had my craw stuffed full of Pythagoras when I was a kid. Mathematics. Pythagorean geometry. And astronomy, too. There, he was mostly full of crap, but he's still regarded as something of a genius in mathematics."

"Ja." Pulvermacher cleared his throat. "But he also taught that maybe a person could pass from one world into another and then go back. Did you ever hear of that?"

"Not in Boston, my friend."

"Ach, nein. But Pythagoras believed in the transmigration of souls. He was an ancient Greek, but even so he could have got the notion from Cathay or India, where the idea is much older. There, the people still hold such ideas. You, I guess, would call it . . . moving from one dimension to another. Maybe that is what this girl you see has done."

Brightlaw only shrugged his shoulders.

Hanrahan or Wolf Call might call it a supernatural phe-nomenon. Pulvermacher had a scientific or analytical ap-proach to it. Either way, nobody knew for sure. And the final answers might not be much different, in any case. . . .

It was well short of noonday when they spotted smoke trees, the first they had seen in a long time, growing in a meandering line a little southward. Brightlaw remembered what Wolf Call had said about the possible proximity of wa-ter to these. He turned the patrol in that direction.

The land all round about had been so effaced by blowing sand that it was impossible to discern any sign of the stream-bed along which the trees would have grown. And now their trunks were half-buried.

Once more Brightlaw had the eerie sense of knowing that they could dig here and find life-giving moisture. No vision appeared to him; nothing out of the ordinary occurred. He felt a solid conviction, that was all, and he pointed to a deep blanket of sand.

"There," he said. "We'll dig right there."

Both Hanrahan and Pulvermacher looked doubtful, and Hanrahan said, "God *damn*, Seth! Are ye so sure, then? Did the Injun haunt tell ye *that*, too?"

"No. It's there. Dig."

Hanrahan grumbled that they might be wasting their last strength on naught, but again Pulvermacher stolidly agreed that they had nothing to lose. Once more the canteen was down to a few small swallows of water. If they were so close to their destination, another full canteen would carry them through.

They dug into the loose sand, heaving out double handfuls, until, only two feet down, they found moist ground and widened out a deep excavation. Both Hanrahan and Pulvermacher regarded Brightlaw with a kind of solemn awe as they waited for the pit to fill, but he couldn't explain it any better than they.

"Wolf Call said it might be," observed Max.

"Shouldn't be so easy, though," grunted Hanrahan. "That spirit, she's touched Brightlaw with her own magic, I think. Made him a little daft. And he not Irish, even!"

Feeling in a better humor, they drank all they could, filled the canteen, and went on. . . .

CHAPTER TWENTY

WHEN THEY CAME ONCE AGAIN ON THE TRACKS OF UM-
berhine's patrol, the sun was much higher.

They were sitting down to consume their last rations when
a sudden desert zephyr, blowing from the north, carried to
their ears a faint popping of gunfire. Heavy shooting, the
shots so crowded that they seemed to overlay each other.

No words were needed now. The three troopers threw
their gear hastily together and headed along the now north-
curving road. It was hard going across the last stretch, where
the road wound like a rugged brown snake between giant
sandstone boulders and clattering canes of ocotillo, the loose
sand whipping in gusts against their faces and bodies.

If they were to run into hostile fire now, their few remaining rounds of ammunition wouldn't be likely to carry them
through another encounter such as their last one. Pray God
that if Umberhine and his troop were just ahead, they would
have enough shells to share. . . .

The winds subsided, dwindling slowly away.

Abruptly, as they came up on a long, rock-littered rise,
lifting their eyes just enough to top it, they saw the cluster of
buildings below: ancient, wind-scoured adobes. The pole-
and-thatched roofs had been partly burned away, no doubt
by fire-arrows. The view offered glimpses of people inside:
the white or varicolored clothing of Mexican peones, as well
as the blue-clad forms of troopers. This must be San Bernardino, a humble hamlet for certain.

Scattered around, in loose encirclement among the outlying boulders, were the crouching brown forms of the Mojaves.

Brightlaw summed it up in a glance: Probably taken by surprise, Umberhine had laid up himself and his command in a conventional barricade of buildings. And the Mojaves, for once assembled in a sizable force, had cunningly encircled them.

"We'll scatter," Brightlaw murmured to his companions. "Get to different positions behind the Indians and lay down a steady fire. They might be tricked into thinking it's fresh troops coming up."

"That's the ticket," grinned Michael Hanrahan. "That damn fool shavetail's got his men bunched together in them 'dobes. They'll not have a chance in hell of busting out, unless we give it to 'em."

"It might work," agreed Pulvermacher. "Wolf Call has told me that all the Indian's training is directed toward not being taken by surprise. If by surprise you take him, you have him where the short hair is."

"Glad we're in agreement," Brightlaw said dryly.

Actually, he knew their chances of bringing it off successfully were probably slimmer than of there being an icicle in Hell. There were too damned many Mojaves, and the three of them had too few shells left.

But what other choice was there? Pinned where they were, Umberhine's men and the villagers would finally be starved out, or perish even sooner for lack of water, depending on how much food or water they had.

"Listen," Brightlaw said quickly, "we've one edge. We've all got Winchesters now. The Indians will expect the usual charcoal-burners, Springfields, in the hands of white troops— one shot before you have to reload. All right. We'll move around some up here—*but stay out of sight if you can*. If they think there's a passel of us, we'll have a better chance. But they'll recover from their first surprise. So fire rapidly, but try to make every shot count. We've none to spare."

It was their single real advantage. The three troopers divided their remaining cartridges equally. Then they separated at the top of the rise. Hanrahan stayed planted on his heels where he was, while Pulvermacher ranged to the right, Brightlaw to the left. Each man was to move no more than a hundred feet either way. Then they were to open fire. Brightlaw's first shot would be the signal.

Brightlaw ducked low among the strewn boulders till he'd found his position. The magazine of his Winchester was nearly full, perhaps a dozen shells in all. Would they be enough?

He shifted his shoulders to limber them, the dirty rag of his blouse chafing the half-blistered flesh beneath it. Only his palms were sweating, and he dried them on his shirt front. After a deep breath, he took careful aim and pumped off two quick shots.

The Indian was a clear target and he dropped like a stone, without making a sound.

Instantly Hanrahan and Pulvermacher opened up from their positions. Not waiting to see the results, Brightlaw loped farther to his left a couple of yards and fired again. This time he hit nothing, but the sudden fire from their backs, the whine of slugs off nearby rocks, had already demoralized the Indians.

The Irishman and the German were firing just as effectively. One Mojave sprang to his feet, only to be knocked spinning by a bullet. Another started to turn, then simply folded up at the middle and went down. Hanrahan and Pulvermacher were switching positions as swiftly as Brightlaw.

The Indians finally realized that they were being attacked at their exposed backs. They tried to scatter to better positions. It meant leaving their present shelter and trying to dodge to other cover . . . only to lay themselves open to the troopers in the buildings. Some of the peones added their own fire, even if less effectively.

A ragged volley of excited yells and cheers went up from the army men and the villagers. Three more Mojaves went down under gunfire from front and back. Meantime the attackers at their backs were fading rapidly from one position to the next, feeding the hostiles' impression that they were at least semi-surrounded.

A half-dozen of them broke and ran, against the raging orders from one man that they stand their ground. Or so Brightlaw interpreted his cries.

Again an impulse sprang unbidden to Brightlaw's mind: Get that bastard—or get his attention now. Wipe him out and you've got 'em all on the run.

Was that something he had heard somewhere . . . or was it what Hanrahan had called his touch of magic? Whatever— he remembered it for a certainty. Kill a leader, the war chief of a party, and the rest were likely to lose heart. To continue the fight would be bad medicine.

Brightlaw drew a careful aim and pulled down on the man. His shot missed, but sent a ricochet whanging off a boulder so close to the war chief that it brought him wheeling around.

How many shots have you left? Brightlaw wondered. He hadn't kept track of how often he'd fired, but the Winchester must be nearly empty.

Got to get him in range . . . if I can.

Brightlaw slipped out between a pair of boulders so that he stood boldly forward on the rise, in plain sight. He raised the Winchester above his head and shook it, letting out a mighty shout.

He was flinging out a naked challenge. And the war chief accepted it.

The Mojave was almost directly below Brightlaw. Even at this distance Brightlaw could see the crazed fury on the war-rior's blue-and-vermilion painted face.

He came sprinting up the shallow rise with an incredible agility, gripping his rifle across his chest. Suddenly he stopped and flung the weapon to his shoulder. He and Bright-law exchanged shots simultaneously.

Both were hasty shots. Both were clean misses.

The Indian came on and up at a fierce, driving stride. Brightlaw let him come, rifle butt still at his shoulder. When the Indian, not over a hundred feet away now, halted to take another aim, Brightlaw fired.

This time the war chief was knocked backward by the bullet's force. He rolled downward a few yards and then crawled back to his feet. He resumed climbing, but now he moved sluggishly, doggedly, his teeth set with pain.

Finish it, Brightlaw thought. He took a careful bead on the spreading stain of blood on the man's shirt.

The hammer fell on an empty chamber. He had used his last bullet. He reversed the Winchester in his grip, clubbing the rifle barrel in both fists. He waited, only dimly aware that the rattle of gunfire below continued its lethal din but was slackening off now.

The war chief came to a stop. Chained to his own code of honor, fearless and stubborn, he threw his rifle aside. He fumbled the knife from his belt and clambered weakly upward.

Man to man. He wants it that way. Fair is fair.

Brightlaw dropped the rifle and pulled his own knife, feeling a twinge of admiration for his injured enemy. Even as the thought came to him, a shot fired by a warrior from below caught him a numbing blow in the right arm.

He stumbled and fell to his knees, then lurched back on his feet. The pain hit then, and he could barely keep his grip on the knife. But he plunged down the slope, digging in his heels.

Fair is fair.

He wasn't over four yards from the Mojave when the war chief made his final violent effort. He surged upward, swinging the knife high above his head. Then he gasped, his eyes rolled blindly, and he pitched forward on his face.

The down-swinging blade drove into the ground less than a foot from Brightlaw's left boot.

CHAPTER TWENTY-ONE

THE MOJAVES WHO WERE STILL ENTRENCHED BELOW THE rise saw how their war chief had died. Now they thought only of escaping this place. They burst into flight, heading for another rise of ground nearby where, presumably, they had left their horses tethered. Two more of them were shot down by the defenders in the buildings before they reached it.

This time they had no opportunity to carry away their dead. The gunfire directed at them was too fierce. Moments later, a clatter of hooves, a billow of dust beyond the farther rise, attested to their quick retreat toward the west. . . .

Brightlaw, Hanrahan, and Pulvermacher descended from the rise and went down to the buildings. They slogged along wearily, just about on their last legs.

The peones were grateful. Men clasped the hands of their rescuers with murmurs of *"Gracias, senores."* Several young and attractive women came up to embrace the troopers, sobbing their gratitude (which might have been fairly enticing under other circumstances).

Three of Umberhine's troop were dead. Several others were wounded, but none of them seriously. The troopers clustered around the three rescuers, shaking their hands and demanding explanations. But they weren't in any shape to offer any just yet.

First Lieutenant Philip Umberhine was lying in the shaded corner of one building. His blouse was off, torn into strips that had been used to bandage his thick torso. He was unconscious now, but blood was seeping through the bandages.

"I don't reckon he's goin' to last long," Line Sergeant Menzies observed in his usual glum, weary manner.

He said it directly to Private Seth Brightlaw, as if soliciting his advice. Whatever their individual ranks might be, it seemed that somehow, unbidden, Brightlaw had been acknowledged the leader of this troop.

"Well, Barney, let's just get things in order for now," Brightlaw said gently. "We'll assume that the siege of San Bernardino has been lifted. I doubt if the Mojaves will gather this way again. We'd best head back for Fort Burnshaw."

Next day, rested up and slept out, the troop began its slow march along its back trail. Lieutenant Umberhine was carried on a litter by men on foot. Other members of the troop who'd been wounded were able to walk or sit their horses. Most of B Troop's mounts had been lost along the way, shot or stampeded during shootouts with the Mojaves.

Up ahead, the troop's former tracks had been erased where the sandstorm had struck. But their head scout, White Hand, would have no difficulty guiding them over the sand-blown trail. A small and wizened man of about sixty, he—like Wolf Call—was a full-blood Cahuilla.

Brightlaw, Hanrahan, and Pulvermacher slogged tiredly alongside each other toward the front of the loosely formed column. They felt a deep, if almost unspoken, comradeship. Still, they said nothing to one another for a long time.

Finally, perhaps inevitably, Brightlaw said, "Mike, we may not be able to locate that buried gold of yours again. Depending on whether Wolf Call is alive or not."

"Aye." Hanrahan was staring at the ground as he walked, plunking down his booted feet as if each bore a leaden weight. "And that'll do it for me, lads. That gold, even divided up with you buckoes, was the key to me future."

"Maybe we will lucky be," said Pulvermacher. "Maybe Wolf Call is still alive. We are not far from the place where we left him.'' He chuckled mildly. ''And maybe his 'medicine' was good, *ja*?''

Brightlaw's head was hot, dizzy, aching. His wounded arm with its cumbersome weight of bandages was in a sling across his chest.

White Hand was ranging out ahead of the troop, and presently he raised a hand to signal a halt. Peering through the dance of heat-veiled air, they saw the lone figure of a man plodding slowly toward them along the ill-defined road.

It was Wolf Call, for sure.

When they met he greeted them solemnly, his stoic face showing none of the pain he must be enduring. He had applied a fresh jimsonweed poultice to his wounds: he had found water where he'd hoped to find it. With all that he also had his tremendous stamina, which equalled that of Hanrahan, who was a good deal younger.

''And can we still find where the gold was buried, laddie?'' Hanrahan asked eagerly. ''I'd like to have me share of it, someday.''

''I find,'' said Wolf Call with the grim trace of a smile. ''When you want to claim it, Han-ran.''

''That might be a spell of time from now,'' Hanrahan said grumpily. ''For me, anyway, I'm going back to face the charge of desertion. But I'll want to divide it among us four, as I promised.''

''White-eyes, you all crazy about gold,'' Wolf Call replied. ''Not so with Cahuilla. But I show you when time come.''

They made an early camp that evening, cooking up their meager rations, eating as much as they could, drinking plenty of water. The springs at San Bernardino had provided enough to fill all their canteens.

Still feeling sick and sluggish, Brightlaw was preparing to settle down for the night when he was approached by Line Sergeant Barney Menzies.

''Seth, Lieutenant Umberhine is awake. He's askin' for you. Wants some palaver.''

"All right,"

Brightlaw tramped wearily across the camp to where Umberhine lay bundled in a cocoon of blankets. His face was pale and drawn, all its usual color drained away.

Brightlaw dropped on his haunches beside him, resting his crossed arms on his knees. "Well, Phil?"

"You won . . . you bastard." Umberhine's voice emerged from his cracked lips as a grating drawl. "I'll be dead in a little while. And you'll have her at last. You'll have Marlee."

Brightlaw sighed and shook his head. "I don't know, Phil."

"You know I'm as good as dead, goddammit! Isn't that enough?"

"Is that what you wanted to palaver about?"

"Maybe."

Umberhine shaped his faint, wicked smile that he remembered so well. And Brightlaw met the glare of unrelenting hate in Umberhine's gaze.

He said quietly: "You haven't changed any, have you, Phil?"

"Not one damn bit. I never could. I hate your guts, Seth. I always have."

"I guess you did at that," Brightlaw said uncomfortably. "I never knew why, though. You won Marlee. You were always the winner. Not me."

"Yeah," Umberhine husked. "Yeah. That's how it looked on the surface. But I was wrong. Maybe I knew it all the time. Goddamn. I do hate your guts."

Brightlaw shook his head wearily. "I'm sorry, Phil."

Umberhine gasped out a long, rasping cough, blinking his bloodshot eyes. "Like so much shit you are."

Brightlaw said nothing. When a man's festering, irrational hatred ran that deep . . . When so much had happened that Brightlaw couldn't wholly explain even to himself . . . There was nothing he could explain to a mind-warped and hate-filled man on the edge of death.

He could wish that things hadn't turned out this way, but

that would be like saying that if wishes were horses beggars would ride.

The troop took up its weary march the next day. First Lieutenant Umberhine, borne along on his litter, passed quietly away about noontime.

A halt was called by Line Sergeant Menzies. They dug a deep grave for Umberhine, and Menzies—knowing what he thought he did of Brightlaw's and Umberhine's friendship in their youth—asked Brightlaw if he'd say a few words over the burial site.

The troopers gathered around, heads bowed.

Brightlaw's speech was brief. His own words tasted sour in his mouth. He kept any reference to religion out of it. He had no idea of what Umberhine had ever really believed, if anything.

The troop continued on its way, heading south and then north along the sand-blown trail to Fort Burnshaw.

CHAPTER TWENTY-TWO

As they neared the tan sprawl of the fort's weathered adobe buildings, built in a rough quadrangle around its dusty parade ground, the men's spirits picked up visibly.

Troopers dropped exhaustedly off their horses, the handful of married ones greeting their wives who came hurrying out to meet them. Mostly they were a drab and slatternly-looking lot of women, even the younger ones. Many of them eked out a living by washing clothes for officers and noncoms, thus supplementing their husbands' meager salaries. But you could sense the brimming love among them—as if Hell itself had flung its furies at them and still hadn't dented some inward dignity.

And where do you stand? Brightlaw silently asked himself as he hobbled across the parade toward the enlisted men's barracks.

Pulvermacher and Hanrahan had dropped back to assist a couple of the wounded troopers. With his good arm Brightlaw took off his battered relic of a hat and swatted it against his pants, detachedly watching the dust fly.

This was no hero's homecoming. It was neither defeat nor victory. It was the bedraggled upshot of nearly all the grubby wars, big or little, that men had ever fought. Nobody had won. *There are no winners, for Christ's sake! Won't they ever learn that?*

Likely not. White or Indian, what did it matter? Something in man made him a hater, a fighter, causing him to excuse his own actions with the bravura of largely empty

slogans. Sometimes Brightlaw thought that all nature, including human nature, was basically amoral; it was all fang
and claw. No explaining it . . .

No explaining, either, the weird images of the Indian girl
who had appeared to him. Had they really lived together in
other lives? Would they live together again? Hell, did it really
matter?

Brightlaw shook his head quickly, sharply.

He knew he was feeling the letdown, the miserable after-
effect of all he'd gone through. His thinking was fuzzy and
uncertain, and he was still feeling the feverish aftermath of
his wound. Before long he would have served out his enlistment period, and he'd be free to take up a new way of life—
but for what?

"Seth! Oh, Seth . . ."

It was Marlee's voice. He turned his head, blinking against
the sun's glare. She was standing in front of the officers'
quarters, wearing a bright gingham frock. She held one hand
half-lifted, and her smile was tremulous, the shine of tears
plain on her cheeks. Her words were soft, little more than a
murmur, yet they reached him plainly.

Brightlaw waved his hat once and plunked it back on his
head, giving the brim a jaunty tap with his forefinger. He
made himself return the smile. She didn't yet know about
Phil, and decorum wouldn't permit her to act more inti-
mately.

But now he had an answer of sorts, all the same. In this
life there was still Marlee. There would always be Marlee.

ABOUT THE AUTHOR

T. V. Olsen is a longtime favorite westerns author who has seen many novels into print, including two, *Arrow In The Sun* and *The Stalking Moon*, which were made into popular movies. He has three times been nominated for Spur Awards by the Western Writers of America. Olsen lives with his wife, who is also a writer, in Wisconsin.